"Dammit, we're practically engaged. If it hadn't been for Susan, we would be by now."

Her heart jumped into her throat. "What do you mean? What are you talking about?"

"You know what I mean. We'll discuss it later. Now, kiss me, dammit."

Without waiting, he pulled her back into his arms and kissed her soundly. He kissed her as if he feared he would never have another chance. His lips burned on hers, while his arms riveted her to him, until she no longer doubted it was she and no one else whom he loved. She felt it in every atom of her being. . . .

By Joan Smith
Published by Fawcett Books:

THE SAVAGE LORD GRIFFIN
GATHER YE ROSEBUDS
AUTUMN LOVES: An Anthology
THE GREAT CHRISTMAS BALL
NO PLACE FOR A LADY
NEVER LET ME GO
REGENCY MASQUERADE
THE KISSING BOUGH
A REGENCY CHRISTMAS: An Anthology
DAMSEL IN DISTRESS
BEHOLD, A MYSTERY!
A KISS IN THE DARK
THE VIRGIN AND THE UNICORN
A TALL DARK STRANGER
TEA AND SCANDAL
A CHRISTMAS GAMBOL
AN INFAMOUS PROPOSAL
PETTICOAT REBELLION
BLOSSOM TIME
MURDER WILL SPEAK
MURDER AND MISDEEDS

MURDER AND MISDEEDS

Joan Smith

FAWCETT CREST • NEW YORK

A Fawcett Crest Book
Published by Ballantine Books
Copyright © 1997 by Joan Smith

All rights reserved under International and Pan-American Copyright Conventions. Published in the United States by Ballantine Books, a division of Random House, Inc., New York, and simultaneously in Canada by Random House of Canada Limited, Toronto.

http://www.randomhouse.com

Library of Congress Catalog Card Number: 97-90254

ISBN 0-449-28791-2

Manufactured in the United States of America

First Edition: October 1997

10 9 8 7 6 5 4 3 2 1

Chapter One

"If I had known it wasn't to be an engagement party, I would not have chosen a theme of hearts and flowers," Sir Reginald said with a moue.

He gazed forlornly down the length of his small, bijou ballroom, which had been transformed into a bower of bliss for the expected betrothal. He had gone to inordinate pains and to great expense to import every flower he could get his hands on, to say nothing of the hundreds of gilded hearts glittering amid the foliage. Not only did flowers festoon the entrance hall and doorways of the ballroom, they even hung, heads down, in nosegays from the ceiling, their stems cleverly wrapped in sodden cotton batting and covered in leaves. Nothing done for Art was too much trouble for Sir Reginald Prance.

His own elegant person, thin as a herringbone, was outfitted in a jacket of violet velvet, to indicate he was in half mourning for the loss of Lady deCoventry due to her betrothal to Lord Luten. He had had his valet trim a handkerchief with violet lace, which he planned to apply to his moist eyes when the announcement was made. In his pocket rested a bottle of hartshorn to evoke the necessary tears.

"A lady can hardly accept an offer of marriage before it is made," Lady deCoventry replied. Her lovely lips did not form a pout. She was determined not to reveal by so

1

much as a blink that she was disappointed at Luten's failure to come up to scratch.

"One cannot but wonder why didn't he offer," Prance mused. "Surely he has been on the edge of it all week. After he saved your life in that extremely harrowing adventure regarding your stolen pearls, you have been especially nice to him."

"Perhaps he would prefer not to marry a widow," Lady deCoventry said, and raised her fingers to cover a well-simulated yawn. She was actually the Dowager Lady deCoventry, the relict of a gentleman old enough to be not only her papa but her grandpapa, to whom her Irish father had sold her for five thousand pounds when she was seventeen years old. After three years of marriage, her husband had conveniently died four years ago, leaving her well provided for.

"Oh, my dear! Surely Luten is not so common. He will screw himself up to the sticking point tonight when he takes you home. He is only flesh and blood after all. You look positively luminous this evening. Who could resist your exquisite beauty?"

He allowed his eyes to play over Corinne's manifest charms. Luten called her Black Irish, whatever that might mean. In any case, her hair was black as a raven's wing and looked delightful against the ivory cameo of her delicately carved face, with those big emerald eyes and full lips. Her toilette, he thought, was not quite up to the standard of its wearer. Corinne had a slight tendency to overornament herself. The diamond necklace was quite sufficient, without that brooch. He blamed this excess on the dearth of garniture available to her in her impoverished youth. But it scarcely mattered, for friends without flaws were boring after all.

"I didn't come with Luten. Coffen will take me home," she said, smiling thinly at her cousin, Coffen Pattle.

"Have the waltzes with Luten," Sir Reginald said. "They will put him in the mood. You must not fail us, my pet. *Tout le monde* is awaiting the announcement."

When Sir Reginald Prance spoke of *tout le monde*, he really meant the particular friends of the Berkeley Brigade. This set of young Whig aristocrats, so called because they lived on Berkeley Square, were the acknowledged leaders of the ton. The nucleus consisted of Lady deCoventry, Prance, and Coffen Pattle, with the dashing Marquess of Luten their unofficial chief.

"Tarsome fellow," Coffen said, rubbing his ear. Coffen presented a surfeit of flaws to endear him to Sir Reginald. His appearance was in sharp contrast to the elegance of the other members. His short, stout body was covered in a rumpled jacket. Even his cravat pin was poorly chosen. His modest pearl disappeared against the white linen of his cravat. Beneath a tousle of mud-colored hair, a pair of blue eyes peeped innocently out from his ruddy face. "Where is Luten anyhow?" he asked, looking around.

"One of his footmen brought him a message a moment ago," Prance replied. "Probably from the House. He went into my study to read it. Some new machinations from Mouldy and Company for us to thwart, no doubt."

"Mouldy and Company" was the Brigade's derogatory name for the reigning Tory government, against which they waged unholy war for reform in the House.

"I hear the fiddlers scraping up for a waltz," Coffen said. "Shall I haul him out of the study?"

"Not on my account," Corinne said with an air of the utmost indifference, and scanned the room for an escort handsome enough to annoy Luten.

Before she found one, Lord Luten himself appeared in the doorway. Prance gazed at him in despair. How the deuce did Luten invariably manage to look so elegant? He spent scarcely a moment with his tailor, yet he turned out magnificently. Nature had given him a head start, of course, and his valet, the inestimable Simon, was an acknowledged wizard. That cravat was absolute sleight of hand. Luten was tall and lean, with a good set of shoulders on him. His jet-black hair grew in an interesting point on his forehead. His cool gray eyes were saved from severity by an enviable set of lashes. His strong nose and square jaw lent him a masculine air, but it was his thin lips that added that lovely touch of arrogance Sir Reg envied, and that Luten was not even aware of. Unconscious arrogance was the very cream of arrogance.

Trust Luten not to come forward, or even to beckon. He just tossed his head commandingly to summon his minions. Corinne ignored him, until Coffen put his hand on her arm.

"He looks worried. Best come along," he said. "It must be important."

"Hurry! I cannot delay supper. My ice sculpture is melting!" Prance exclaimed, and darted forward. Cupid's bow and arrow were very fine. He should have settled for a heart, but it was too pedestrian.

"What's afoot?" Coffen demanded, when they reached the doorway.

"Susan's been kidnapped," Luten said in a hollow voice. After shooting this verbal cannonball at them, he turned and retreated to Prance's study. The others looked stupefied for a moment, then hurried after him and closed the door.

Prance had kept a rein on his originality in this serious chamber. It was a severe room with oak paneling and the usual desk, chairs, and cabinets. A gentleman needed one room in which he could play at being a serious man of affairs. Luten sat on the corner of the desk and the others stood around him.

4

After the first stunned silence, Corrine asked, "When? How did you find out?"

"A note from Jeremey Soames came to my house a moment ago. As it was marked 'urgent,' my butler had it sent here."

"What does Soames want you to do?" Prance asked.

"He doesn't say, but of course, I shall go to Appleby Court at once." His eyes darted uncertainly to Corinne.

Prance looked around in alarm. "Tonight? But my party—"

"A lovely party, Reg. Sorry I must leave, but Susan—"

"I'll go with you," Coffen said.

"Yes, of course, we must all go," Corinne said. "Little Susan is like a sister to me," she added hastily, lest Luten take the absurd notion she was going on his account.

To say Susan was like a sister was a slight exaggeration. Corinne's mind roamed back to the past. She had spent her year of mourning at Appleby Court, in East Sussex, after her late husband's death. It was there that Luten had proposed to her, three years before. And she, like a fool, had rejected him. She had wanted a period in which to enjoy her new freedom. His pride had been sorely bruised. The refusal had led to three years of snipping and sniping between them, before the affair of the stolen pearls had brought them together.

There had been a strange sequel to her refusal. In a fit of pique, he had turned around and offered for his cousin, Susan Enderton, who had also refused him. That bizarre week sometimes seemed like a dream, but it was no dream that Luten was terribly upset at Susan's being kidnapped. His lean face was pale and drawn. Was it possible he really loved Susan? That his offer hadn't been made in a fit of pique, but that he had loved her all this time? Was that why she, Corinne, hadn't received the expected offer tonight?

5

When she turned her attention again to the conversation around her, she realized she had missed a good deal. Prance was saying, "I can't leave my own party. It would be too outré, but I shall join you and Pattle at Appleby Court tomorrow."

Coffen said to Luten, "The rest of us can go together—you, Corinne, me."

Again Luten glanced at Corinne, then quickly averted his eyes. "I'm taking my curricle. It's faster," he said. "It only seats two. You can come with me if you like, Pattle."

"What about Corinne?"

"She could come tomorrow with Prance, if she feels it necessary to come at all."

"I shall go tonight," she said, glaring at Luten.

"I'm not sure that's a good idea," he replied. "A lady can't be much help. Just one more to worry about, with a kidnapper on the loose."

Her Irish temper broke. "Susan is like a sister to me," she repeated. When Luten lifted his well-arched eyebrow in derision, she added, "I expect I know her better than any of you. A lady is more likely to notice little details amiss."

"I am quite as familiar with Susan as you or anyone else," Luten said.

"What sum do they ask for her return?" Coffen asked.

"Soames didn't mention it, but her dowry is twenty-five thousand. I expect whoever snatched her is well aware of it."

Coffen squeezed his face into a frown. "By the living jingo, we must find her before the money is handed over. Twenty-five thousand! I'm off."

"It was a lovely party, Reggie," Corinne said, pressing his fingers. "Sorry we must dart off."

"Say no more," Prance said with a wave of his white

fingers. "Naturally Susan's safety must take precedence over a party." It did seem hard, but he had to maintain his reputation for exquisite manners and sensibility.

Since it seemed there would be no wedding arrangements to engage his talents, he would amuse himself by finding Susan, and perhaps instigating some romance between her and Luten, to vex Corinne. The rogue in him enjoyed these games. Ill natured, but there you were. He, too, had his flaw. He drew his lace-edged handkerchief between his fingers, then raised it to his nose to inhale the delicate scent of lavender water—not Steakes, but a superior brand smuggled in from France at an inordinate price.

Chapter Two

Prance followed his guests to the door to see them off. Luten lived just two houses up the street, in the grandest mansion on the block. Corinne lived directly opposite Luten, with Coffen next door to her. Before crossing to her own house, she said to Luten, "I know you don't want me to go, but—"

Luten lifted an eyebrow and said ironically, "But Susan, whom you haven't seen in three years, is like a sister to you."

"She has often visited me. And I shall go to her now, in her time of need."

"Very noble, but I would prefer to rescue only one lady at a time. You have already used up your turn, Countess. You will recall that the shortest route to Appleby Court is via Hounslow Heath, a well-known haunt of highwaymen. If you must come, wait until morning."

The butler handed him his hat; he reached out his hand and took it without looking at the man, placed it on his head, allowed his cape to be dropped on his shoulders, his cane put in his hand. Then he turned on his heel with a great flurry of the cape and strode out without saying good-bye.

"I must remember that exit for our next *drame*," Prance said, smiling fatuously. "Shakespeare's famous

'Pursued by a bear' is nothing to it. 'Possessed by demons' is more like it. Even when he is in a state of distraction, one can always count on dear Luten for that touch of the theater in his doings." He offered Corinne his white fingers, where an amethyst the size of a small cherry twinkled. "I shall be with you anon, dear heart. Promise you won't find Susan before I arrive."

"Let us go, Corinne," Coffen said impatiently. "Mind you don't wear any jewels or take much money with you. Highwaymen. I mean to tie my blunt up in a handkerchief and stuff it into the toe of my boot."

"That is the first place the scamps look," Prance informed him.

"In the crown of my hat, then."

Prance sighed wearily. "That cunning hiding spot will take them all of three seconds to discover. I have a false bottom built into the seat of my traveling carriage."

"There's not time to rebuild the carriage," Corinne said. "I must change and pack a few things. We'll take some footmen to act as guards."

Coffen turned to Prance. "Pity you can't come now. We'd be safer with another carriage along. The scamps are less likely to attack a caravan."

Prance gave little thought to actually rescuing Susan Enderton. He weighed the delights of his party against the frightening pleasure of darting through Hounslow Heath by moonlight. When he considered the amount of time and money invested in his party, and the delightful consternation he would cause when he announced Susan's kidnapping, he said, "Too farouche to shab off. I must stay here to keep an eye on things."

Coffen nodded. "Looks like it is only you and me, Corinne. Shall we be off? If we hurry, we might catch up with Luten. That'll be two carriages. And Luten is a famous shot."

"My blessings on you, children," Prance said. He found nothing worthy of emulation in their exit as they scuttled across the broad flagstoned pavement to Corinne's small but elegant yellow brick mansion, protected by an iron railing.

Before parting, she and Coffen discussed the details of the trip.

"Will you bring Ballard with you?" Coffen asked. Mrs. Ballard was Corinne's companion, an obsequious cousin of her late husband.

"No, there can be no impropriety in my visiting Appleby without a female companion. I am a widow after all, not a green girl, and you know they aren't accustomed to much company at Appleby. The trip should not take more than three hours."

"I wager Luten will be there in two. He seemed pretty cut up, didn't you think?"

"Yes," Corinne said, and fell into a silent pondering.

Luten's state suggested that he was in love with Susan. If he were to marry anyone other than herself, then Susan was about the only lady Corinne could approve of. She was sweet and innocent, unlike Luten's usual high flyers. Susan had just turned seventeen that year after deCoventry's death, but her provincial upbringing made her seem younger. She had looked to Corinne as a model, asking questions about London and beaux and balls. Mrs. Enderton had been alive then, but she was a country lady and could not give Susan the sort of information the girl wanted. Corinne had not been exactly a second mother to the girl, more like an older sister.

When Mrs. Enderton had died, Susan had taken over as mistress of Appleby Court, with her mama's brother, Otto Marchbank, handling the estate business. Corinne had visited Appleby Court twice, and Susan had visited her three or four times in London—but not for some time now. It must be a year since her last visit. How quickly the time flew! Could Susan have found a beau in the last twelve months? Her beauty, her sweet disposition, and her dowry of twenty-five thousand would have made her entirely desirable. Could it be her cousin Jeremy Soames? It was he who had written to Luten.

"Will you be ready in an hour?" Coffen asked. "I'll have to pack and send for my traveling carriage. I'll take my team of four. Fitz won't like being roused out of bed at such an hour." Coffen's groom, indeed all his servants, had their master firmly under their collective thumb. His house was pretty well run for their convenience.

Remembering the highwaymen, Corinne said, "Tell Fitz to bring a pistol."

"Since that time we was held up right in London, I always make sure there is one under the coachman's box."

Corinne darted into the house, calling to her butler as she ran, "Send Mrs. Ballard up to me at once, if you please. I am leaving for Appleby Court immediately with Mr. Pattle."

Black was not surprised at the trip, but he was surprised that her ladyship had left Sir Reginald's party so early. What occurred to Black was that one of her chums had become involved in a duel and was being smuggled out of town before the law got hold of him. Someone had made a slighting remark about her ladyship, very likely. Her friends would not allow that to go unpunished. This being the case, Black was highly desirous of accompanying his beloved mistress to Appleby Court to see her name was avenged. Sir Reginald Prance, he fingered for the likeliest one to be caught up in a duel. Coffen was too good-natured and Lord Luten too sensible, despite his toplofty ways.

"I can dress myself, Mrs. Ballard," Corinne said when

her mousy companion came bustling into the bedroom. "I want you to have a small trunk brought down from the attic. Pack me a couple of muslin dresses—my new rose sprigged and the blue one. And one—no, two gowns for evening wear. I shall not be going out or entertaining."

As she spoke, she removed her jewelry and pulled off the jonquil-colored gown she wore. "Will you put my jewels away for me? I shan't be taking any with me."

When she explained where she was going, Mrs. Ballard said, "I'll pack your good cashmere shawl. Many's the evening I have sat shivering in that drafty place. But won't there be any parties? Miss Susan is at that age—"

Corinne daubed at her eyes and said in a choked voice, "She's been kidnapped, Mrs. Ballard."

Mrs. Ballard gasped in alarm. "Oh my goodness. The poor child! I did wonder at your setting out in the middle of the night. That would be why Lord Luten's footman went darting out of the house. He was going for the carriage."

A sound of horses and wheels in the street caught Corinne's attention, and she went to the window. Luten's shining yellow curricle with silver appointments stood at his front door now. Even as they spoke, Luten came pelting out and hopped into the driver's seat, while his tiger handed him the reins. He had not stopped to change out of formal clothes, nor to have Simon pack a change of linen. His valet would be following then, in the closed carriage.

"He will find Susan, milady," Mrs. Ballard said. "Now, dry your tears. I will ask Black to make you up a nice cup of tea while I pack your trunk."

Corinne changed into a green worsted traveling suit while her trunk was being packed, then went below, just as Black came up from the kitchen with the tea tray. He revealed his eagerness to accompany her, but the offer

12

was declined. Coffen made excellent time. She had taken only one sip of her tea when he arrived at the door, sweating at every pore.

"I figured if I rushed, we might join up with Luten," he said.

"Too late. He has already left."

He gave a longing look at the tea, said, "We'd best be off, then," and rushed her out the door.

Chapter Three

While the footmen secured her trunk to the roof, she and Coffen studied his map and chose their route.

"Looks like the Great West Road to Twickenham Road and on to Hampton Court Way is our best bet. It will take us right past Hounslow Heath, but there's no avoiding it. I have left my cravat pin at home and wrapped my blunt up in this handkerchief," he said, showing her a knotted piece of muslin.

"Susan made this handkerchief for me," he continued, gazing at it fondly. "Gave half a dozen of them to me for my last birthday. The cloth is a little funny. Seconds, she called it. Something went wrong in the weaving, but as it was stitched with her own dear fingers, I treasure it."

Corinne had encouraged Coffen Pattle in his laggardly pursuit of Susan. She thought they would make a good pair, both so friendly and undemanding. She had believed that nothing had come of it, but if Susan had sent him a birthday gift, perhaps she'd been mistaken.

"Should you not cut a slit in the lining of your hat and hide the money inside?" she suggested.

"What, destroy my hat? It's one of Baxter's finest curled beavers. I value it as much as the blunt I'm bringing. I'll just hold the hankie in with a pin. You wouldn't happen to have a pin on you?"

"No."

"Then I will put it under my shirt, hold it in the pit of my arm if we are stopped. Where have you hidden yours?"

"In different places—pockets, the toes of both shoes. I folded some bills under the ribbon of my bonnet and some in . . . more private places."

"Ah, in the top of your stocking. I hope they don't look there."

"I doubt he will find all my hiding places. And I am wearing this little glass brooch that I don't mind losing. He might mistake it for a diamond and be content with that. We'll have footmen riding with us as well."

"Just one, I fear. The others didn't care to come," Coffen said sheepishly. "I asked Raven—my valet, you know. I would like to have him along, but he don't care for travel. Young Eddie will ride with Fitz on the box."

When the trunk was stored and the driver given the map, Coffen called, "Spring 'em," and they were off.

The trip out of London was executed with no problems. Once beyond the bustle of the city, the road stretched dark and menacing before them. A fingernail of star-dogged moon floated high overhead. It did not even begin to dissipate the shadows. When they reached the deserted heath, a tension crept into the carriage. Coffen sat with his eye trained out the left window, while Corinne peered out the right side. A low-lying fog curled close to the ground, with darker forms of shrubs and an occasional tree protruding above. At one point they entered a tunnel of trees. A breeze moved the leaves with a soft, hissing sound.

"This is where he'll get us," Coffen said in a tense voice.

"Stop it, Coffen. You're making my flesh crawl."

In the darkness of the coach, a ray of moonlight caught the gleam of metal from his pistol.

"Don't point that thing at me," she said.

"It ain't loaded."

"Coffen! You came without loading your pistol! What is the point of that? Charge it at once."

"I didn't have any bullets at home. I thought the gun might scare him off." He heard a distinct sigh of frustration.

"I hope Fitz and the footman have loaded guns," she said.

"Just told you, I didn't have any bullets."

They soon came out the other end of the tree tunnel, fortunately unscathed, and continued their perilous journey. Once they were clear of the heath, the worst of the trip was over and they could devote their worries to Susan. Appleby Court lay in a sheltered glen of the weald at the northern edge of Ashdown Forest. As they drew near, the farms and estates were familiar to them. When they heard the clatter of hooves come thundering out of a meadow, they took it for some local buck on his way home from his late night revels. Even when the rider cantered alongside their coach, they felt no real fear. It was not until a shot rang out and the driver slowed to a stop that they heard the fatal words, "Stand and deliver. You two, on the ground, facedown." The carriage lurched as the driver and footman followed orders. One lone masked rider suddenly appeared at the carriage door, leveling a pistol at them.

Corinne sat, frozen as a statue with fear, clutching at Coffen's sleeve. It was the second time she and Coffen had been held up in his carriage. But on the other occasion, the coachman's gun had been loaded, and he had managed to scare the thieves off.

"This is it," Coffen said in a hollow voice. "If I don't come out of this alive, Corinne, I want you to tell Susan . . . well, you know. Very fond of her. Love her, in fact."

With this heartfelt speech he opened the door and stepped out, holding his left arm suspiciously close to his chest. His coachman and footman were already on the ground, facedown.

"The lady as well," the rider ordered. He pitched his voice low to conceal his normal speaking voice.

Corinne felt sick with fright. She was by no means sure she could stand, but somehow she got out and stood, clinging to Coffen for dear life, while her heart throbbed in her throat. She noticed that Coffen had forgotten to bring the uncharged pistol with him, which was perhaps just as well. A pistol might frighten the highwayman into firing.

"Take off your hats and shoes and hand them up to me," he ordered, and they complied. With one hand he examined Coffen's hat and tossed it aside. Then he took the bills from beneath the ribbons of Corinne's. While they removed their shoes, she tried to gauge the highwayman's size and shape, but as he never dismounted, it was difficult. Every inch of him except his hands and chin were hidden, by either hat, clothes, mask, or boots. Neither hands nor chin were unusual in any way. He wore no distinguishing rings. If he walked into her saloon the next day wearing no disguise, she would not recognize him.

"Shake them out," he ordered.

They both shook their shoes. When the bills fell out of Corinne's, he ordered her to pick them up and give them to him. "I'll have the brooch as well, milady."

She unpinned the brooch and handed it to him. He ran one finger around its edge, felt the roughness of glass, and tossed it aside. Then he cocked his pistol at Coffen.

"No one travels this light. Your money or your life, sir," he said, in a voice that raised goose bumps, although

17

it was perfectly civil. Perhaps it was the pistol, aimed at his victim, that made the whole affair so terrifying.

Coffen felt cold all over, as if his heart had turned into a block of ice. He reached into his shirt. The handkerchief had slipped down to his waist. He fished it out and tossed it to the man, who caught it with his left hand, weighed it in his palm, then stuck it in his pocket.

"A pleasant journey to you both." He kicked his heels into the flanks of his dark mount, tipped his hat, and galloped off in a thunder of hooves.

Coffen and Corinne exchanged a frightened look, then drew a deep sigh of relief.

"No point going after him," Coffen said. "By the time I had a nag unharnessed, he'd be miles away."

"Let him go. It's only money." They picked up their hats and brushed the dirt from them.

"Not much I could do, when the pistol was unloaded," he said.

"I'm glad you didn't try anything foolishly heroic— but next time bring a loaded pistol. I wonder if he got Luten as well."

"No such luck. Not that I wish Luten ill, but there's no denying a few knocks would do him the world of good."

While they talked, the groom and footman got up off the ground and came forward.

"He just seemed to come from nowheres," Fitz said apologetically. "I made sure we was safe once we got clear of the heath."

"It's not your fault, Fitz," Corinne said. "He didn't harm you?"

"No, milady. I picked up this rock ready to heave if he touched you." He held out a largish rock.

"That was well done," she said. "We had best continue on our way before another of them comes along." She glanced around the ground, but seeing no sign of the brooch, she left it there. They recovered their shoes and took them into the carriage to put on there.

"I still have ten pounds in my stocking," Corinne said, as the carriage rattled along the now familiar roads. "How much did you lose, Coffen?"

"Fifty and my watch. It'll leave me short, no denying."

"It's not much to pay for our lives."

"That's true."

They sank into a companionable silence, each thinking of their close call, and inevitably of that other time they had been robbed. A few lights still burned as they approached the village of East Grinstead. The first building of note was the Rose and Thistle, a half-timbered inn and coaching house. A small knot of people stood in the yard, apparently waiting for a stagecoach. A man straggled on unsteady legs through the deserted village.

"Foxed," Coffen said.

Somewhere a dog barked.

On the far side of the village they passed Oakhurst, the estate of Jeremy Soames, Susan's cousin who had written to Luten. It was all in darkness. Oakhurst was a small estate and not very profitable. Soames had sold his land on the other side of the road, which was an apple orchard. The blossoms had fallen, leaving traces of petals on the ground. As they drew close to Appleby Court, they passed a little farm called Greenleigh, owned by a yeoman farmer, Rufus Stockwell. The lower story was in darkness; a light beamed in one bedroom abovestairs.

It was one-thirty when they reached Appleby Court. The iron gate standing between the stone pillars was open. A long sweep of pebbled drive curved in a graceful circle to the house. Luten had taught Corinne and Susan to drive on this road. There by that big elm he had proposed to her—and perhaps to Susan as well. And now Susan was gone, kidnapped. It didn't seem real to

19

Corinne. Surely when they opened the door, Susan would come flying out and throw her arms around them.

From halfway through the park, she could see the general outline of Appleby Court. Its pale stone stood out against the darkness. It was not a palatial house designed by some famous architect but a big, rambling three-story building that had grown over the generations with more attention to use than beauty. A light burned in the saloon window. Someone was still up, then. That was good. She could certainly do with a cup of tea.

She wondered what Luten would say when he heard they had been attacked by a highwayman. She was not an ill-natured lady, but she secretly hoped, with Coffen, that the highwayman had got Luten as well, or they would never hear the end of his "I told you so's."

Chapter Four

"I told you to wait and come in the morning!" Luten exclaimed when they finally roused him up from the sofa to answer the door. His tone displayed disgust, yet he was aware of a leap of pleasure to see that Corinne had come running after him. It would be the devil of a nuisance having her here at this time, but a constant worry if she were in London without him. He would just have to make sure that she didn't discover certain details about his recent doings with Susan.

"We are fine, thank you. I am sure your failing to inquire for our safety does not intimate a lack of interest," Corinne said, and strode into the saloon. She sat on a faded sofa that rested on a faded Persian carpet, facing a pair of faded velvet window hangings, once blue, now a dusty, opalescent gray. The cold grate across the room seemed a symbol of their cheerless welcome.

"I can see you are safe," Luten said. "I assume you managed to traverse Hounslow Heath without incident."

Coffen lowered his brows at Corinne. "We're here, ain't we?" he replied.

Corinne wanted to frighten Luten with the tale of their attack, but to spare a lecture, she said, "What have you been doing to find Susan?"

"Resting, so that I might have an early start in the morning."

21

"After darting off from the party like a madman, you didn't bother to speak to Soames?" she asked.

Luten seldom apologized, but he did deign to explain. "His house was in darkness when I passed. It seemed uncivilized to disturb him."

"Surely manners take second place when Susan's life is at stake."

"You are not in Ireland now, Countess. Manners are always in fashion in England." She was only Countess when Luten was angry with her. Recently she had been elevated to Corinne.

"Don't be tarsome, Luten," Coffen said. "You knocked at his door and there was no answer."

Luten shrugged his elegant shoulders. "If you say so."

"I hope he ain't out on the road, or the highwayman— a highwayman might get him," Coffen said, and turned as pink as a peony.

Luten cast a steely gray eye on the new arrivals. "The highwayman? Don't tell me you've been robbed again!" He flashed a quick, worried glance at Corinne, to confirm that she was unharmed. He saw her small smile of satisfaction at the unwitting gesture and turned at once to examine Coffen. He noticed the dusty rim of the curled beaver on the sofa. "And you hid your blunt in the lining of your hat. Why not just hand it to him on a platter?"

"I did nothing of the sort! I had it hidden under my shirt. The wretched fellow threw my hat in the dust for nothing. I believe his mount must have stepped on it." He picked it up and brushed at it. "And it was my favorite hat, too. If Fitz had had the pistol loaded as he ought to—"

Luten rolled his eyes ceilingward and murmured, "Spare me." Then he turned again to Corinne. His sharp eyes darted over her body from head to toe, looking for signs of violence. Finding none, he said in a thin voice, "I trust you had the wit not to carry your jewelry nor any

22

considerable quantity of blunt in an unguarded carriage at night, Countess?"

"You will be happy to learn he took the little glass pin you have so often disparaged."

"Did you report it at East Grinstead?"

"No," she said shortly. "Actually, I am not that fond of the brooch."

"Damn the brooch! You shouldn't have left the man running loose to attack other travelers. You should have told the local constable."

A sense of guilt lent a sharp edge to her reply. "I doubt Hodden even has a mount, let alone the courage to go after the scamp or the cleverness to catch him."

"The scamp didn't bother you, Luten?" Coffen asked.

"No, he didn't."

"Perhaps he wasn't in the mood for a lecture," Corinne said.

"I'll tell Hodden tomorrow," Coffen said, and looked at the cold grate. "We could do with a few logs."

"And a cup of tea," she added.

"Feel free to help yourselves." Luten wafted an elegant hand toward the fireplace. "There is the grate. There are no logs, though any of this lumber is fit for the fire," he said, eyeing the furnishings askance. "The kitchen, one assumes, is belowstairs."

"I take it the servants have retired?" Corinne asked, reining in her temper.

"I caught the butler on his way to bed. Tobin was kind enough to provide me with this horse blanket," he said, nodding to the sofa, where he had been resting. An uncomfortable-looking bolster was at one end, a dark blanket, though not actually a horse blanket, at the other.

"Where is Mr. Marchbank?" Coffen asked.

"He was in his study, drunk as a lord, when I arrived. Tobin and I got him upstairs to bed. There is nothing we can do before morning. Tobin tells me the beds are not made up, but if you prefer an unmade bed to the floor, then I suggest you find a candle and go abovestairs."

Corinne looked all around the saloon. "The place has gone to rack and ruin!" she exclaimed. "I have not been here for some time, but it was not this bad when last I was here."

"That was at Mrs. Enderton's funeral," Luten reminded her. "It seems our Susan takes little interest in home-making."

"I've been here since then!"

"Shockin'," Coffen said, and strolled off to the dining room in search of wine and glasses.

"So you have not learned anything in all the time you have been here?" Corinne asked Luten.

"The half hour by which I preceded you is well accounted for."

Coffen returned with the wine and handed around glasses.

Luten took a sip, then spoke. "Tobin tells me Susan disappeared yesterday afternoon. It was fair day in Grinstead. Otto—Mr. Marchbank—was at the fair. Susan told the housekeeper, Mrs. Malboeuf, that she was going to the orchard to do some sewing. It seems she often did so."

"She made me half a dozen handkerchiefs for my birthday," Coffen said. "The demmed highwayman got one of 'em."

"She took her sewing basket with her," Luten continued. "When she did not return for dinner, Tobin went in search of her. She was not there, nor was the sewing basket. She hasn't been seen since. Around eight that evening, Otto reported it to the constable, who has been searching the area and asking questions since that time. None of the neighbors saw her. There were, of course, several strangers in town on a fair day. The thinking is that one of them spirited her off."

"Has Marchbank received a ransom note?" Corinne asked.

"No." A frown pleated Luten's brow. "That is rather odd."

"Then if this man who took her was not after money . . ." Corinne stopped as the significance of this sank in. "She is very pretty."

"The bounder!" Coffen exclaimed.

Luten worried his chin with his thumb and forefinger. "There would be any number of pretty girls at the fair, some of them available for a pittance. It is unlikely a lecher would go after a lady, knowing the consequences would be severe. I still hope there will be a demand for ransom."

"He had a lot of gall, going right into her orchard," Coffen said. "And how would he know about her going there? You don't figure it could be a local lad?"

They all exchanged a sapient look. "You are referring, I collect, to Baron Blackmore?" Luten asked. "The same thing occurred to me. He would be happy to get his hands on her fortune. If he forced her to spend the night at his house, she would be obliged to marry him, hence the lack of a ransom note. He'd bring her back to Appleby as his bride, a fait accompli."

"He's had her long enough to fait accompli her. Why didn't he bring her home?" Coffen asked.

"We must go and rescue her at once!" Corinne said, rising.

Luten gently pushed her back onto the sofa. "Blackmore was at the fair. The devil of it is, all the local suspects were there."

"Who would these chaps be?" Coffen asked.

"First and foremost, Blackmore. Then there is Soames and that Stockwell fellow from Greenleigh."

"Soames wouldn't kidnap her," Corinne said. "When she refused to come to London to make her debut, I figured she was going to accept an offer from Soames."

Luten's gray eyes focused on her with bright intensity. "Did she intimate anything of the sort?"

Corinne noticed his sharp look and felt sure it was jealousy that caused it. "No, but she had no interest at all in coming to London, and you know how she used to talk it up. She could hardly wait to get there."

"We shall speak to Soames in the morning. And Blackmore," Luten said.

"And Rufus Stockwell," Coffen added.

"And Rufus," Luten agreed. "There is little we can do tonight. I suggest you find yourselves a bolster and a couple of blankets and tuck in. We shall be up and about early."

"Up with the fowl," Coffen said, frowning at the thought. "I could do with a bite to eat before we hit the tick."

Luten yawned, covering his lips with his raised hand. A carved emerald glowed on the small finger. "It takes longer than twelve hours to starve to death, Pattle."

Coffen frowned at his protruding stomach. "Where are we to sleep?" he asked.

"I have no idea." Then he turned a mischievous eye on Corinne. "Unless you would like to share my sofa, Countess?"

"Is there no bed of nails available? That would be more to my liking."

"That is my cue to offer you my sofa and find myself another bolster." He rose and gestured toward the sofa with a wave of his arm.

"I wouldn't dream of discommoding you, Luten,

26

knowing you put your creature comforts above all else—
even manners. I expect Susan's bed is made up. I shall
sleep there."

On this setdown she left the room, to see her trunk had
been deposited in the hallway by Pattle's groom and
footman. To have it taken abovestairs would cause too
much racket, so she removed her nightwear and a muslin
gown for morning and went upstairs. The stairway was
dimly illuminated from the hall below, but once she
reached the second story, she was plunged into darkness.
Rather than return below for a lamp, she felt her way
along the hall, counting doorknobs. Susan's room, she
remembered, was the third one on the left. When she
opened the door, a faint ray of moonlight gave enough
illumination to show her the lamp and tinderbox. She lit a
lamp and gazed around at the familiar room.

It had not deteriorated as badly as the rest of the house.
Although Appleby Court belonged to Susan, she had not
removed to her parents' grander bedchamber upon her
mama's death. Her belongings were still in the room she
had used as a girl. It was not part of the nursery, but had
been decorated in a manner to please a young girl. The
wall was covered in light paper decorated with apple
blossoms. The carpet, though worn, still showed a pattern of pink flowers. The furnishings were dainty ladies'
pieces, painted a creamy shade and trimmed with gilt,
similar to those in Corinne's bedchamber in London.
Susan had disliked canopied beds. She imagined mon-
sters were hiding in the curtains. Her mama had removed
the hangings, leaving the four posts bare. Susan had used
the posts at the end of the bed to hold two of her straw
bonnets.

Corinne turned to the desk, thinking there might be
some clue there. She smiled to see the volumes of
Camilla resting on the desk. She had sent Susan the five

27

volumes for her birthday, thinking she would enjoy the romance. She noticed that volumes one to three were there. Presumably Susan was reading volume four, and it was somewhere about the house. It was odd, though, that she had taken volume five with her as well. Corinne was a little surprised to see Byron's *Childe Harolde's Pilgrimage* on the desk. A little risqué for Susan ... She opened the cover and read, "To Susan. Many happy returns on your birthday. Love, Luten." She might have known! How exactly like Luten to send a young girl such a book. She frowned at the casual "Love." He usually signed any note to herself "Sincerely" or "Your servant."

She was suddenly overcome with fatigue. She turned down the counterpane, happy to see the bed had not been stripped. She undressed and climbed gratefully beneath the covers, where she lay awake for a long time. Hunger gnawed at her, but it was not what kept her awake, nor was it the strange bed. Where could Susan be? Was she even now confined by some lecher such as Blackmore, being forced to give herself to him? Or worse, was she already dead, killed by some raving lunatic? Why had there been no demand for ransom?

Her mind wandered over her friendship with Susan. The girl was as helpless as a kitten. And a good deal friendlier. If some man who looked like a gentleman asked her for directions, she was as likely as not to go along with him in his carriage to show him the way. It was so dreadfully easy for a trusting girl—child, really—like Susan to be kidnapped. Yet Susan was no longer a child. She was now twenty years old.

This being the case, it was odd she had allowed Appleby to fall into such disrepair. Was it possible Otto had lost her money in bad investments? He drank a good deal. If that was the case, then a ransom demand could not be met. She and Luten and the others must pitch in and raise the required sum. But perhaps her money was intact. Susan had no notion of household management. Her mama had done all that sort of thing. If they found her—*when* they found her—she would have a talk with Susan about keeping up Appleby Court.

Would she marry Blackmore if he was the one who had carried her off? Mrs. Enderton had warned her and Susan away from him during her mourning visit here. "Not fit for decent company," she had said, so Corinne had very little knowledge of him. What a wretched husband he would make an innocent girl. Would Jeremy Soames have her if she had been ruined? In any case, Susan must not marry Blackmore if she did not care for him. Surely she didn't care for him—although he was rather handsome, in a horrid, sinister way, like a villain in one of Miss Radcliffe's gothic novels. That wastrel would squander her estate in no time.

Susan would be better off a spinster. At least she would be independent. It was lovely being independent, as long as one had enough money for some of life's little luxuries. Corinne had never thought, when she was at home in Ireland, that she would ever be in her present position—still young, still healthy, and now wealthy to boot. An accepted member of the most Haut Ton group in London, the Berkeley Brigade. If they all hung together, they could get Susan accepted in Society, whatever ill had befallen her. Coffen, for instance, would still marry her. Perhaps even Luten . . .

She frowned and turned over to begin counting sheep. When she opened her eyes, sunlight streamed in at the window. Dancing sequins of iridescent light reflected from the mirror onto the ceiling. At least the weather wasn't going to hamper their search for Susan.

Chapter Five

From her bedroom window Corinne looked out on a perfect picture of bucolic peace. This picturesque corner of East Sussex, nestled amongst the woods and moorlands, seemed the last place on earth one would expect violence and possibly even murder. The branches of tall trees moved lazily in the breeze. Graceful swallows cut a swath against the brilliant blue heavens. In the distance a raucous daw protested some grievance.

Corinne turned reluctantly from the window and began to dress for the day in the older blue muslin she'd got from her trunk the night before. After a hasty toilette, eager to get on with the job, she went downstairs.

She was annoyed to find Luten his usual well-groomed self when she went to the morning parlor for breakfast. There had been no warm water for her to make a toilette. She had pulled the bell cord in vain and finally used the cold water in the basin in Susan's room. Yet Luten had obviously shaved. He wore an immaculate cravat and had not slept in that jacket he wore either.

Luten's cold eyes raked her from head to toe, then lifted again to frown at her hair. He performed an exquisite bow. As he drew her chair, he murmured softly in her ear, "Setting up to play the role of Lady Medusa, Countess?"

Her temper rose, but she replied coolly, "Has your valet arrived, Luten?"

He gestured gracefully at his waistcoat. "As you see. If Simon cannot take care of me properly here, I shall remove to the Rose and Thistle. You ought to have brought Mrs. Ballard with you. You look, if you do not mind my pointing it out, as if you had combed your hair with a rake."

"Thank you. I did not mistake that 'Lady Medusa' for a compliment."

"Your gown could do with an ironing as well," he added, eyeing it with disdain as he took up a chair opposite her.

"We have more important things to think about than our toilettes."

"Surely we are capable of managing two thoughts at a time?"

"Have you learned anything since last night?"

"I had no revelatory dreams, if that is what you mean. Since rising, I have learned that Mrs. Malboeuf makes a demmed poor cup of coffee and cannot fry an egg for toffee. Your stormy eyes tell me you are still concentrating on your one thought. Regarding Susan, I have already milked Tobin dry. Otto continues to sleep it off. I have asked Tobin to send Mrs. Malboeuf to me when she finishes burning your toast and bacon. Ah, here she is now. Lucky you!" he added sotto voce, as a plate of scorched toast was slammed onto the table in front of Lady deCoventry.

"Do yez want eggs?" the dame inquired in a bellicose voice.

The woman was nothing else but a slattern. Her gray, flyaway hair was nominally held in place by a cap. Her apron, once white, looked as if an artist had used it to clean his brushes. It held all hues, from brown gravy

31

splatters to berry juice to something vaguely green. Mold, perhaps. Her enormous bulk suggested that eating was her major function in the kitchen. Her heavy face was set in a mutinous expression, giving her the air of a bulldog.

"No, thank you," Corinne said, "but I would appreciate it if you would make up a bedroom for me."

Mrs. Malboeuf placed her hands on her battleship hips and said, "Dora is gone, isn't she? How am I expected to clean the house *and* do the cooking?"

"Gone where? Do you mean she disappeared with Miss Susan?" Corinne asked.

"Gone two months ago. Run off to Burnham with one of the grooms from Slattery's stables. She *says* they're married. I hope it may be so, for the kiddie's sake."

Corinne refused to follow up this teasing statement. "Why did you not replace her?"

"I'm not the one holding the purse strings. Servants like to be paid," was her curt reply.

"And are you paid for your somewhat minimal services, Mrs. Malboeuf?" Luten inquired, with a civil smile.

"I was, last quarter day."

"Then we can assume dire poverty is not the reason for the state of things here. That can wait until later, however. We want to ask you a few questions regarding your mistress's disappearance."

"I already told Mr. Marchbank and repeated it to Hodden and Mr. Soames. She took her sewing basket out to the orchard right after lunch on Monday and never come back."

"How did she seem when she left? Did she behave in any unusual manner?" Corinne asked.

Mrs. Malboeuf drew a sigh and stood, giving the

32

matter deep thought. "I thought it odd she wore her blue muslin," she announced, after a long pause.

Luten blinked in confusion. No color was so becoming to Susan's blond hair and blue eyes. "Why did you find that odd?"

"It was brand-new, wasn't it? Why would she go to sit on the grass—and it had rained the night before, too—in her new gown? Plus she wore her pearls and new kid slippers. If you want my opinion, she was meeting someone. A man," she added, to make her meaning perfectly clear. "And it wasn't the first time she'd got herself all dolled up to go out to the orchard either. Made quite a habit of it since the weather hetted up."

"She took nothing with her but her sewing basket?" Luten asked.

"She took a piece of plum cake on a plate. The plate was found, empty, though she told me earlier the plum cake was not to her liking. Pretty sharp about it being a little burnt on the bottom. That stove—"

"Have you any idea who it was she met there?" Corinne asked hastily, to forestall a litany of complaints.

"No. I haven't time to go running after her. That's not my job. With Dora gone and only Peg to help out, I've got my hands full and then some. You'll find a man at the bottom of it, is all I'm saying. No good comes of a lady loitering about an apple orchard. Look at what happened to Eve."

"Surely you misconstrue the Bible, Mrs. Malboeuf," Luten said. "It was Adam who was so heinously ruined by Eve in the Garden of Eden."

"That's as may be. It's Miss Enderton as is missing, not Adam. Aye, there was a serpent there waiting for her, mark my words. I've no use for an apple, tart it up as you might. I suppose you'll be wanting linen for the beds?"

"You spoil us, Mrs. Malboeuf," Luten replied. "Preferably clean linen, if it is not too much trouble."

"I ain't a laundress. Miss Enderton never replaced the washing dolly when it broke down either, though I asked her a dozen times. Pretty sharp with me about that as well, the last time I mentioned it. I scrubbed her sheets by hand on a washboard. My poor knuckles are raw."

"We take your word for it," Luten said, "but pray do not bother to make the beds up with soiled linen. My valet will make some arrangement with the inn. I understand all the gentlemen of the immediate neighborhood were at the fair on Monday. You did not see any of them lurking about Appleby Court?"

"No," she said, somewhat regretfully. "They all say they was at the fair, and it seems innocent folks have supported the story."

"Thank you. You have been very helpful," he said.

She strode off, her hips jiggling like jelly.

"I wonder why Susan has let things go so dreadfully," Corinne said, shoving the cold toast aside. "Do you think Mr. Marchbank has lost her money?"

"That is the obvious explanation. I shall look into it as soon as Otto comes down."

"It sounds as if something was bothering Susan. Mrs. Malboeuf mentioned a few things—you know, about Susan speaking sharply to her, complaining of the plum cake and washing dolly. That is not like her."

"She would have to be an angel not to complain of that slattern's work. She ought to have done more than complain."

"But she never used to complain about anything, is what I am saying."

"What do you make of her wearing her new frock?"

"It does sound as if she was meeting a beau, does it not?"

34

"I am not a lady, Countess, which is why I am asking for your opinion. For myself, I try to make a pleasing appearance at all times."

"You might try to please with more than your appearance, Luten. A gentleman's manner is also important. It seems odd she would wear a new gown to a damp meadow just to read *Camilla*."

Luten's fine brows rose in a question. "Why do you assume she was reading Fanny Burney? She was supposed to be sewing."

"Susan hates sewing. She did sew a little, just to pass the time, you know. The last two volumes of *Camilla* are missing from the set I gave her. The first three are in her room. I wager she took the others with her."

"That is an odd way to entertain a lover—to read to him. And not even romantic poetry, but one of Fanny Burney's tedious tomes of overwrought romance in five volumes."

"Fanny Burney is more appropriate to a girl of Susan's years than Byron's poems. That book you sent her was quite inappropriate, Luten."

"She particularly asked me for it."

"I didn't realize you were in correspondence with her," Corinne replied in a stiff way. "She never mentioned it."

"There is no need to wear that Friday face, Countess. I would hardly call it a correspondence. There was nothing clandestine in it, if that is what you imply. She wrote to wish me a happy birthday and was kind enough to enclose a gift." Corinne looked at him, wondering if he would expand on it. "A pair of slippers she had knitted for me. I was touched, despite the dropped stitches, and asked what I might send her for her birthday. She said I must not even think of such a thing, then mentioned her grief that Byron was not available at the lending library

35

in East Grinstead. You know how cleverly ladies insinuate these things without actually saying them. I took her hint. She never thanked me for the gift, by the by, but perhaps next birthday I shall receive another pair of slippers to keep the blue ones company in my dresser."

Corinne wondered at that lengthy explanation, so unlike Luten. Almost as if he felt guilty. "Well, I am shocked," she said indignantly.

"Yes, one would have thought Byron would be available, even in East Grinstead."

"I mean shocked that you would send her that book. Very likely that is what incited her to go meeting some rake in the orchard."

"We don't know that she was meeting a beau. For that matter, *Camilla* contains its share of romantical intrigues. A good deal more than its share. But we are not here to criticize each other's taste in literature. Let us examine Susan's room. There might be a billet-doux from this elusive lover hiding in the pages of *Childe Harold*, or even *Camilla*."

They left breakfast on the table and went abovestairs. While Luten riffled through the desk, Corinne searched the clothespress to see if any of Susan's gowns were missing. When Luten saw what she was about, he said, "Tobin tells me there is nothing missing save the gown she wore on Monday."

"Perhaps there is a billet-doux in one of her pockets."

Luten looked as if he wanted to stop her, but he didn't say anything. She wondered, then, if he had chosen to search the desk by chance, or did he expect to find something—something he preferred that she not see? She watched him from the corner of her eye to determine whether he secreted anything.

Susan's pockets held a comb, a small hand mirror, an illustration of a very dashing gown from a lady's magazine, and advertisements for Austrian foam soap and a violet scent, but no billets-doux. Again Corinne was surprised. Susan had never taken much interest in such things as fancy soaps and scent. To carry a mirror in her pocket suggested a new vanity as well. And that gown in the illustration was a good deal too daring for Susan.

When she turned toward the desk, she noticed Luten had moved on to a chest in the corner. "That only holds extra blankets," Corinne said.

Luten lifted the lid, glanced in, and closed it again. "Let us go and have a look at the meadow," he said.

"We haven't looked in her dresser drawers," she said, and went to take a quick look. "That's odd."

"What is it?" he asked in a tense voice.

Corinne held up a ball of wool and knitting needles. Three inches of pink knitting hung from the needles. Its shape left some doubt as to whether it was the beginning of a scarf or was to be shaped into slippers. Half the stitches had slipped off the needle.

"She seems to have dumped this here in a great hurry. She used to keep her knitting in that big straw sewing basket she took to the orchard."

"Let us go to the orchard," he said.

Corinne had a sense he was rushing her out of the bedroom. She gave the rest of the drawers a cursory search but found nothing of interest.

Coffen was at the table, sullenly chewing his way through the burned toast, when they returned belowstairs. He looked like an unmade bed in his wrinkled jacket. His lower face was shadowed in whiskers.

"You aren't fit to be seen in public," Corinne scolded.

"Sorry, but there was no hot water, you see, and I've not been able to find my trunk."

"There is no pleasing the wench," Luten said aside to Coffen. "She chided me for being too neat."

Coffen took no interest in sartorial matters. His major concern was always his stomach. "They don't set much of a table here," he said. "I spent the night in an armchair, dreaming of beefsteak, and woke up to charred bread. I plan to take a drive into East Grinstead to report the highwayman. I'll ask some questions about Susan as well and take lunch at the Rose and Thistle."

"Do bring us back a crumb," Luten implored. He told Coffen what they had learned and surmised thus far.

"Rubbish," Coffen said. "If she had a beau, she would bring him to the house."

"Not if he was ineligible, if Mr. Marchbank disapproved," Corinne said.

"The only ineligible gent around is Rufus Stockwell, from Greenleigh," Coffen said. "We ought to have a word with him, though I think that Blackmore is a likelier customer. Except that he was at the fair. So was Stockwell, come to think of it, and Soames. I wonder if there were Gypsies about the neighborhood."

"Now, that is something we did not ask Mrs. Malboeuf," Corinne said to Luten.

Luten gave a supercilious smile. "Despite my flighty way of thinking of more than one thing at a time, I asked Tobin when I spoke to him. No Gypsies. I fear Fanny Burney would be quite bored with Susan's tale. And now, if you will excuse me, I must have a word with my valet." He bowed and glided off.

"He is not taking all this very seriously," Corinne said.

Coffen pushed aside the charred crusts and said, "He is, really. It's just his way to show off. He can't help it."

"We were supposed to be going to the orchard to look for clues. I daresay he is arranging his evening toilette instead. Conceited ass. I shall go and examine the orchard myself. And you, Coffen, must make Mrs. Malboeuf boil you some water for a shave before you go to the village."

"I will. She can't burn water."

They enjoyed a short gossip. Corinne told Coffen about the notes exchanged between Susan and Luten. "Do you think there is still something between them? You remember he offered for her once."

"There's no knowing with Luten. He'd not say a word until he was sure she'd have him. I always figured it was you he had in his eye, but he didn't come to the sticking point for Prance's party. There's no gainsaying he was very eager to come flying to Susan's rescue. Do you know what he said to me last night after you left?"

Corinne felt a little pinching at her heart. "What?" she asked, in a fearful voice.

"He said, 'I would give anything to have her back.' And he sounded as if he meant it. *Anything.* I was shocked."

"They have been writing to each other and exchanging small gifts. She knitted him a pair of slippers."

"Slippers, eh? That looks bad."

"But she made you handkerchiefs."

"Aye, a hankie is more personal, somehow. Mean to say, you put slippers on your feet. Nothing romantic in that, whereas you blow into a hankie."

Corinne hardly knew what to say to that. "Well, I am off to the orchard. I cannot wait all day for Luten to join me," she said, and left.

Chapter Six

The warmth and sun were pleasant after the damp gloom of the house. The silence was peaceful, too, after the racket of London. Corinne left by the front door to avoid Mrs. Malboeuf. She skirted the side of the house to the rear, through the walled garden, where tender fruit trees were espaliered against the brick, which held the warmth at night. Beyond was the home garden, with vegetables neatly laid out in rows. At least someone was tending the garden. Carrot tops formed a lacy ruff of green, with peas and beans climbing up their stakes beyond. She and Susan used to pull a handful of baby carrots, wash them in the rain barrel, and take them to the orchard to nibble while they talked.

They had been happy, carefree days, despite the fact that she was recently widowed—perhaps because of it. After the first shock of George's death wore off, she felt free of a great burden. She had liked her husband, but romantic love was impossible between people of such disparate ages.

The apple orchard was to the east. From a distance the trees looked like giant green umbrellas. As Corinne drew closer, she saw that all the blossoms had fallen, forming a withered carpet on the ground. The fruit had not yet set. Susan's favorite spot was in the middle of the orchard where one tree had died, leaving a grassy oasis. Corinne went slowly into it, looking all around. It was a lovely, peaceful spot.

"No one can see us here," Susan had said once. "This is where I hide when Mama is angry with me. If I stay out long enough, she stops being angry and becomes worried instead, then she doesn't scold."

Corinne had smiled dotingly on this artless speech. Susan looked like a little Renaissance angel come to life, with her crown of golden curls, her blue eyes and dimples. How could anyone scold her or be angry with her for long? But actually there was a streak of slyness even in the child. Had it grown to deceit in the young woman? Had she met some ineligible lover in her secret hiding place in the orchard and run off with him?

The grass underfoot was long and still damp with dew. After a rain it would have been quite wet. Susan had not come here to read—but she might very well have braved the damp to meet a lover. The long grass had been trampled, suggesting that Susan did still visit this spot. Corinne began a close investigation, pacing back and forth, covering every square inch. She hardly knew what she hoped to find, unless the lover had dropped some small item that could identify him. A cravat pin, a watch fob, even a button would have been welcome. Or better, a needle and thread, to suggest that Susan had actually come here to sew.

There was an occasional rustle in the branches over-head, but Corinne thought nothing of it. The birds were busy feeding their nestlings in this spring season. One noisy robin in particular made such a racket that she suspected he had a nest close by. She peered up through the branches, wondering if she might spot it, and saw a pair of human eyes staring down at her through the leaves. A strangled scream issued from her throat. Before she could take to her heels, Luten dropped from the tree to land on his feet beside her.

"You frightened the life out of me! Why are you hiding in trees like a hedge bird?" she exclaimed.

"Hedge birds do not hide in trees, but in hedges. Like you, I am looking for clues."

"You must have seen me here. Why did you not say something?"

"I didn't want to frighten robin redbreast any more than I already had. His nest was not a yard from me on the branch. They're quite aggressive when they have birds in the nest. He might have pecked my eyes out."

"Why did you climb the tree in the first place? Surely if there are any clues, they will be on the ground."

"Now, there you are mistaken, Countess."

"I'm sure you are about to enlighten me."

"It doesn't do to keep one's eyes forever on the ground. You should raise them higher from time to time."

As he spoke, a large rectangular object fell from the branch and hit him on the back of the head. He uttered a mild profanity, but was more annoyed than hurt.

Seeing this, Corinne said, "Nature abhors a vacuum," and laughed.

Luten gave her a foul look and picked up the object. It proved, upon examination, to be a straw sewing basket nearly two feet long and half as deep and wide.

"Susan's sewing basket," Corinne said.

"Brilliant deduction, Countess. I spotted it in the tree, but it was wedged in the fork of a branch. It seems I managed to work it loose."

The lid of the box was open, revealing a pink satin lining. The box was perfectly empty.

"How did it get up there?" she asked in confusion.

He turned it this way and that. "It doesn't appear to

have wings. I deduce it was carried up, to conceal it. I further deduce that Susan wouldn't climb a tree in her best gown."

"Perhaps not in a new gown, but she used to scamper up that tree like a monkey. I wonder what happened to her sewing things—needles and threads and cloth. Or was she using it as a knitting basket? That knitting in her dresser . . ."

"I deduce that she either carried some other item here in the basket and removed it, or brought an empty basket with her to fool Mrs. Malboeuf as to her reason for coming to the orchard."

"How very odd!"

"Intriguing. As you are a lady well versed in romantic lore— Don't scowl, my pet. Did your mama never tell you your face might freeze in that mold? I meant only the romantic lore of fiction. What I was about to say was: What do you think a lady might have smuggled out of the house in a sewing basket of this size? If I were writing the book, it would be an illegitimate infant, but one can hardly hope for that."

"This is Susan we are discussing, Luten, not one of your ladybirds. She might have used it as a bandbox to carry a change of clothing, but then why leave the box behind?"

"You are suggesting that Susan ran off voluntarily?"

"Not really. You asked what the box could contain. It could have contained clothing."

"Or it could have contained some item from the house that was too large to hide in a pocket."

"What do you mean?" she asked, frowning.

"If she was short of money, she might have been arranging to pawn some silverplate."

"It is her silverplate. She did not have to hide that she was taking it."

43

"Or she might have been smuggling food out to someone who was hiding for some reason."

"She might have been giving the man the silverplate to pawn and not wanted anyone to know about it," Corinne added.

"You think it was a man, then?"

"She did wear her new gown and best kid slippers."

"And pearls," Luten said, "which suggests a romantic interest in the gent. I must have a talk with some of the local folks to discover if the neighborhood has any scandals floating about. Perhaps some young dasher has killed his man in a duel, or an officer might have deserted his regiment. Something of that sort."

"But if you're implying Susan ran off with him, Luten, she would have taken more than would fit in a bandbox."

"And any money she could lay her hands on as well, I should think." He looked around the little oasis.

"The grass is well trampled," Susan mentioned.

"Yes, before I entered I checked and noticed it was flattened where she would have approached from the house. Let us see if we can discover which way she left."

"And which way the man came in, if there was a man," Corinne added.

They paced the perimeter of the oasis. The grass was disturbed in a few places, due to rabbits perhaps, but the most noticeable place was at the north end. In spots it was possible to see what might have been the actual outline of a shoe in the long grass.

"It looks as if she was alone," Luten said.

"Perhaps the man was carrying her," Corinne suggested. "The grass was wet, you recall."

"Is that how Miss Burney would arrange it? More likely he had knocked her unconscious."

"I should like to know what fiction you read, Luten.

44

Illegitimate infants and ladies knocked on the head. It sounds bad enough to be Monk Lewis."

"Surely you mean exciting enough?"

They followed the path out of the orchard, where it ended in a cow pasture.

"Stockwell's place is over yonder," Corinne said, pointing into the distance.

"So is the closest road, if we eliminate the road in front of Appleby Court," Luten said. "I am assuming the intention was to avoid being seen from Appleby Court."

"This is all conjecture," Corinne said impatiently. "The wind might have flattened the grass, or rabbits or foxes or dogs or a casual trespasser."

"True, but one must conjecture with something. No bricks without straw." He lifted the straw basket, hoping for a smile, but got none. "The sewing basket tells us she was in the orchard. She left, either voluntarily or otherwise, and one assumes she did not fly, but left some trace of her passing. I shall speak to Stockwell."

"He might know about the scandal you mentioned earlier," Corinne said. "Let us walk. It is not far through the meadow."

"Us? Why waste time? You should examine the house, see if silverware or any other valuables are missing. I'll speak to Stockwell. He is hardly the sort of person you should call on. Not quite a gentleman."

"Don't be ridiculous. He is nearly a gentleman. He owns five hundred acres, and I have heard nothing against his character."

Luten considered it a moment. "As I will be there, I daresay it will not look too farouche. We shall drive, however. I know your habit of trotting over the bogs on foot in the old country, my pet, but you are a foin lady now and must try to behave like one."

"Faith and bejabbers, laddie, I never seen such a thing

as a carriage till I come to England. What a grand treat it will be to sit me poor old bones in one."

It was at such moments that Luten felt a pronounced desire to box Lady deCoventry's beautiful ears. She paid no heed to his satirical digs; she never had, but only exaggerated them—and him—into risibility.

"Come along, then," he said curtly.

"We were supposed to be going to the orchard together, Luten," she mentioned. "Why did you slip off without me? You said you were going abovestairs to speak to Simon."

"I did have a word with him. When I came down, you weren't waiting in the hall. I thought you had come on without me."

"I was with Coffen in the morning parlor." She hesitated, wondering if she should mention that Coffen had told her what Luten had said about giving *anything* to get Susan back. She decided against it. Luten obviously had secrets, and she knew the futility of asking him questions. He would only get on his high horse and give her a setdown. She wondered, too, if the word he had had with Simon was to give Susan's room a good search before they returned. He had been in a great hurry to get her out of the room and to search that desk himself. What did he think was there?

When they stopped at the stable to have the curricle harnessed, they discovered that Luten's traveling carriage had arrived.

"Thank God," he said. "My trunk and a few footmen will be here. Armand knows his way around a kitchen. We might have a luncheon fit to eat after all."

"How did Simon get here?"

"He rode my mount. I knew I would need his services before the others arrived, and I felt the mount might come in handy."

Luten's sporting carriage and team of grays, like everything he owned, were top of the trees. The couple were soon flying down the road with the wind on their faces and the fresh greenness of spring meadows flashing by. Sleek cattle grazed in Greenleigh's lush meadows. Greenleigh was a farmstead around an old stone house with a lead roof. It was neither large nor beautiful, but it was in excellent repair. The windows gleamed in the sunlight. Fresh paint shone on doors and window frames.

They drove to the well-ordered stable, where a boy looked up from brushing the horses to relieve Luten of the reins.

"I'll give your bloods a brush-down, sir. A dandy pair of tits."

"Thank you, lad," Luten said, and tossed him a coin.

Luten and Lady deCoventry walked back to the front door, where the shining acorn knocker soon summoned the housekeeper. Mrs. Dorman was all that Mrs. Malboeuf was not. She was clean, tidy, thin, polite, and helpful.

"Mr. Stockwell is upstairs," she said. "I'll fetch him, if you'd care to step into the parlor, milord—and milady. Could I get you a cup of tea?"

With a memory of the turbid coffee they had had for breakfast, Corinne said, "That would be lovely. Thank you."

In a few minutes they were joined by Rufus Stockwell. Corinne had seen him from a distance before, usually mounted on a dappled mare. She had never actually seen him at close range until this moment. He might have been carved from marble by Praxiteles and brought to vibrant life by some latter-day Pygmalion. From the tip of his flowing blond curls to the toe of his top boots, he was a perfect model of young manhood. And on top of it all, he was disarmingly shy. His blue eyes did not quite dare to meet hers. A rosy flush rose up from his open collar. He did not wear a cravat, but his shirt was spotless. He was still arranging his jacket, which suggested he had donned it in honor of their call. The jacket bore small resemblance to the work of the better London tailors, but it was adequate.

When he smiled, a glint of white teeth showed, and when he spoke, his accent, while provincial, was by no means uncouth. "I am honored at this visit," he said, bowing uncertainly. "You are here because of Miss Enderton's kidnapping, I collect?"

"Precisely," Luten replied. "We have ascertained she disappeared from the apple orchard. The markings in the grass suggest she came—or was brought—in this general direction. I wonder if any of your servants happened to see her, or indeed if they spied anyone lurking nearby the Monday she disappeared. A carriage stopped in the roadway, perhaps? Or even a mount?"

"You already know she was brought in this direction? That is clever of you, milord. But I fear none of my people saw a thing. I was at the fair myself. I questioned Mrs. Dorman and the stableboys and the farmhands. I am sorry to say none of them can help us."

"There is one other avenue of query," Luten continued, and asked about any gentleman who might be hiding from the law or an army deserter.

Again he met a dead end. "There has been nothing like that," Mr. Stockwell said, shaking his head. "This is a quiet little place."

The tea tray—a decent silver one—arrived. "I meant to serve you some honey cake, but found it was all gone," Mrs. Dorman said.

Mr. Stockwell said, "I'm sorry, Mrs. Dorman. I worked late over my books last night and helped myself to it before retiring. My housekeeper makes a lovely honey cake," he said, blushing.

The guests expressed a polite disinterest in cake. Corinne poured the tea. She was so delighted with Mr. Stockwell that she accidentally splashed Luten's tea into his saucer. He glared but said nothing. Stockwell leapt forward with his napkin to mop it up, apologizing as though it were his fault.

"The really odd thing," Luten continued, "is that there has been no demand for ransom. You don't think Miss Enderton might have run away?"

"Because of Blackmore, you mean?" Mr. Stockwell asked.

"What do you mean by that, Mr. Stockwell?" Corinne asked in alarm.

"Why, it is no secret old Marchbank wanted her to accept Blackmore's offer."

"Good God! We heard nothing of that."

"We have not actually spoken to Otto," Luten pointed out.

"In his cups again, was he?" Stockwell said, shaking his gorgeous head. "Pity. It is really a shame the way things are run at Appleby Court since Mrs. Enderton's death." He looked a trifle disconcerted after this speech. "Servants' gossip, you know. I do not visit at Appleby, nor does Miss Enderton call on me. It was Mrs. Dorman who told me of Blackmore's offer. Who might help you is Mr. Soames. He and Susan were . . . very close."

"Indeed!" Luten exclaimed.

"Oh yes. I believe there was an understanding between them a month ago. No public announcement was made, however."

"We must call on Soames," Corinne said.

The guests soon rose to leave. "If there is anything I can do to help, you have only to ask," Mr. Stockwell said as he accompanied them to the door.

While he exchanged a few last words with Luten,

Corinne glanced around the hallway. A Chinese urn holding umbrellas was just inside the door. Beside it rested a pair of badly knitted slippers in blue wool. Unlike Luten's, they were not secreted in a drawer but held the shape of their owner's foot.

"That was a fairly futile visit," Luten said when they were outside.

"I would not have missed it for a wilderness of monkeys," Corinne replied.

The stableboy led the curricle out, and they began the trip back to Appleby.

"You found Rufus handsome, I expect?" Luten asked, with an air of indifference.

"I have never met such a handsome man—outside of novels, I mean. And so shy. We can stop imagining that Susan was haring after some other man. With a neighbor like that, she would not waste her time."

"Despite his manifold charms, however, Stockwell is not eligible," Luten said stiffly.

"Because he is not a gentleman? What prevents him from being a gentleman, Luten? He owns land, he is well spoken and well mannered. Is being a gentleman only a matter of birth, of ancestors?"

"That comes into it, certainly."

"Well, given a choice, I would rather be Mrs. Stockwell than Baroness Blackmore. And so would Susan, I daresay."

"Speak for yourself. As to Susan's preference, I trust she has better taste."

"Then you failed to see the pair of slippers in the front hall? Blue, knitted."

"I expect Mrs. Dorman knows how to knit," he said woodenly. "In any case, we can acquit Stockwell of having abducted Susan, I think. I noticed he always called her Miss Enderton and did it quite naturally. A

50

'Susan' would have slipped out if he were accustomed to calling her that."

"Oh, certainly. Mr. Stockwell seemed very proper in every way. So gentlemanly," she added mischievously.

"Not quite in the mold of your usual flirts, Countess. You usually prefer Black Irish, *n'est-ce pas*? Rufus, I rather think, has some Teutonic blood in his veins."

"Or perhaps Scandinavian. Those blue eyes and broad shoulders belong on a Viking," she said, and sighed deeply.

When he did not reply to this taunt, she said, "We really must call on Soames. She gave me no hint that she was interested in him. Did you hear anything of it?"

"I don't believe it was serious. I expect Stockwell has only Soames's version of that so-called understanding."

"Do you think Marchbank was trying to force her to have Blackmore? If that is the case, she might have run away. She would certainly run to us for help, either you or myself. Perhaps she is even now on her way to us in London."

"She had ample time to reach London before we left. She has been missing since Monday afternoon. Soames's letter did not reach me until late Tuesday evening. Her carriage is not missing. One assumes she would have taken her own carriage."

"Well, it is very odd."

"She was kidnapped," Luten decided. "Susan would not put me—us!—and Otto through the anxiety of running away."

Corinne gave him a knowing look and said, "But why has there been no ransom note?"

"Perhaps there has, by now."

He whipped up his team and was back at Appleby Court in minutes.

Chapter Seven

Mr. Marchbank had finally arisen by the time Luten and Corinne reached Appleby. Like the house, he had deteriorated sadly since Corinne's last visit. His hair had faded from gray to white, while his nose had blossomed into that ruby brilliance commonly known as a whiskey nose. He had always been a gruff, unpolished gentleman, but at least he used to make some effort to present a tidy appearance. On this occasion he had shaved and brushed his hair, but the hair was in sore need of barbering. The condition of his shirt was, perhaps, due to the broken washing dolly that Susan had not bothered to have repaired.

He met his guests in the saloon, where he sat with a bottle of wine before him and a glass in his hand. He was still sober enough to rise and shake their hands. At this close range, his eyes betrayed the enlarged veins due to drink.

"Ye've come about Susan," he said, shaking his head. "A terrible business. I hardly know which way to turn. I asked Soames to send for you, Luten, but with the house the way it is, we're not prepared for company. Ye'd be better off at the Rose and Thistle."

"We're not here for a holiday, Otto," Luten said, in a more sympathetic voice than Corinne had expected. "Have you any idea where she could be?"

Again he shook his head. Tears dimmed his eyes, and when he spoke, his voice was unsteady. "Nay, I fear some lecher has carried her off, for a prettier gel there never was, and so friendly. 'Twas fair day, you know. I've been hoping to get a letter demanding money, but none has come. That looks bad, does it not?"

"There is money to pay, should a demand come?" Luten asked.

Marchbank looked surprised at the question. "Aye, there's her dot of twenty-five thousand and a little something besides that has built up in interest. We live simply. I've been after her to fix the place up, but she hasn't her mama's knack for it. She is happy to sit with her nose in a book or magazine. I've been looking for someone to replace Mrs. Malboeuf. She was supposed to be temporary when Mrs. Acton retired, but we never found anyone suitable. Susan's money is in Consols," he said distractedly, hopping from subject to subject. "Do you think I ought to cash them in to be prepared? How long do you figure it would take to get the money?"

"For such an emergency, a bank would take them as collateral and give you the cash at once, I should think. You might have a word with your banker here and make sure he has that much cash on hand. In a small village like East Grinstead, it might take him a day to accumulate twenty-five thousand."

He shook his head. "To see her dowry fly away in such a manner. What sort of husband can she hope for without a dowry? Well, that is something I can be doing, going to the bank. It's the waiting that kills you. Where could she be?" He dropped his head in his hand and sat, a very model of anguish.

"We'll find her," Luten said, with more sympathy than conviction. "Is there any chance she ran off with a beau?"

Again Otto looked surprised. "She doesn't have one. She had an offer from Blackmore, but she put her little foot down at that."

"Stockwell seemed to think Jeremy had offered for Susan."

"It never came to an offer. Susan walked out with him for a week or so, but she found she couldn't care for him. He began telling her how she should run Appleby and that she should hire a house in London and such things. He's a climber, I fear, but he was fond of her. He thought to please her, no doubt."

Corinne listened with interest. "How did he take it when she turned him off?" she asked.

"He was pretty cut up about it, but he settled down in the end. Where can she be? Susan would not be so cruel as to run off without a word to her old uncle and all her friends. She is a good, kind soul, despite her little ways."

Had Jeremy, in a fit of anger, kidnapped her to bring her to heel? No, it was too implausible.

"How did Blackmore take being rejected?" Corinne asked. "Is it possible he might have abducted her? Had her kidnapped, I mean, as he was at the fair that day himself."

"I doubt he'd go that far. It's not as though he were mad for her. 'Twas her blunt he had in his eye, I believe."

"But if he is in dire need of blunt . . ." Luten said, and looked a question.

"He ain't. He was short last winter when he offered, but he came into an inheritance from some aunt in Scotland and has begun repairing his estate. No, money seems no object to Blackmore these days. He bought a new carriage and team this spring, and speaks of going to London in the autumn Little Season to find a bride. No one who knows Susan would harm a hair of her head. It has to be a stranger who has got hold of her. He might have taken her off to London or Scotland or America by now. Will I ever see my little niece again?" he asked, with tears starting again in his eyes.

Luten saw that the man needed something else to occupy his mind, and said, "Let us go into your study to go over the accounts. We should take the Consols to Grinstead and arrange for the ransom, should it be necessary."

"I sit, waiting for a message to come. What is he waiting for?"

When he reached for the bottle, Luten said gently, "Come, let us go, Otto. The note might have come by the time we return."

Otto rose slowly, like an old man. He was only fifty-five, but he looked twenty years older.

After they left, Corinne went up to Susan's room to search the desk and for a closer examination of the whole room by daylight. If the desk had contained any secrets, Luten or Simon had gotten them. She noticed a shawl thrown over the window seat and lifted it. Beneath it sat Susan's writing box. It was a lap box, broad and shallow, whose lid provided a writing surface when no desk was available. The marquetry lid was done in woods of various colors forming a star pattern. Susan must have sat at this recessed window, gazing out at the park, as she wrote.

Corinne lifted the lid and saw two of her own letters and a note from Luten sitting on top of the embossed stationery. Perhaps his birthday letter to her. Was this what he had been looking for? She resisted the temptation to open it, but did examine the envelope. The postmark was only five days old! Susan's birthday had been a month ago. Luten had written to her that recently and not said a word about it!

Had Susan replied to the letter? The lap desk gave no answer. Her wandering eye happened to fall on the

55

wastepaper bin by the desk. It appeared to be full of discarded silver paper, wadded up in a ball. Corinne removed it and saw beneath some smaller papers. She took the basket and emptied it on Susan's bed. A few sheets of stationery had been squashed up and tossed out. She began flattening them. Three of them held a date at the top, the date indicating they had been written a week ago. The salutation, "Dear Luten," was followed by a few lines of script. The actual message was so brief, it was hard not to catch the whole at a glance. "I am writing to ask you . . ." A blob of ink accounted for the letter's having been cast aside. The other two were no more informative. "You must not scold me, dear Luten . . ." and a drop of what looked like cocoa. The other said, "You said I could always turn to you if I had . . ." There was no apparent reason why this one had been abandoned, no smear of ink or cocoa.

Corinne puzzled over them, wondering what Susan had done that might merit a scold from Luten, before turning to root through the other discarded papers, mostly wrappers from the sweet shop in Burnham. Susan had a sweet tooth. This done, Corinne turned back to the lap-top desk and sorted through the loose papers there.

There were two lists. These did not seem too personal, and she glanced through them. It seemed Susan had more interest in keeping up her house than Otto suspected. She had listed various items: carpets, window hangings, a Regency desk, and a chaise longe, with the price of each beside it. The other list was for articles of clothing: bonnets, gowns, silk nightgowns, a satin peignoir with lace panels, petticoats, various pieces of lingerie. The prices listed beside the nightwear were rather high. There was a strange emphasis on intimate apparel. It might almost be a trousseau. . . . Corinne glanced again at the abandoned letters to Luten, with a frown forming between her eyebrows. "You must not scold me, dear Luten . . ." What could it mean? "You said I could always turn to you if I had . . ." It was an ambiguous statement. Was Luten playing uncle or lover?

She went to Susan's dresser to see if she was actually short of nightwear. She had three lawn nightgowns and three flannelette ones. On the back of her door hung a quite nice woolen dressing gown, blue to match her eyes. There was no summer dressing gown. Her eye fell on the blanket chest, and she lifted the lid. There, carefully wrapped in silver paper, were some of the items on the list. A peach silk nightgown with ecru lace was there, along with an assortment of dainty lingerie, all packed in silver paper. And tucked amid the silken folds, a yellow tea rose, pressed between the pages of a book of poetry by Mr. Wordsworth.

Corinne remembered Luten looking in that trunk last night and closing the lid hastily, implying there was nothing of interest there. Was it possible he and Susan were secretly engaged, that he didn't want her, Corinne, to see the trousseau? That was surely what these items were. Luten had sent her Byron's poetry—had he sent her the Wordsworth book as well? She opened the fly-leaf, but there was no inscription. There floated through her mind Luten's pale face when Prance told them of Susan's kidnapping. He had said, "I must go to Appleby Court at once." "I would do anything to have her back," he had said to Coffen. The dramatic phrase was unlike Luten.

She felt a heaviness around her heart, a sense of regret, almost of betrayal. Luten and Susan. When had this romance developed? Was it the affair with Soames that had nudged Luten into repeating his offer? Was that why she had jilted Soames? Why had they kept it a secret? Corinne thought of Susan as almost a sister, but she was

57

beginning to realize she didn't know her at all. Casual remarks that people dropped didn't sound like the Susan of yore. She had "put her little foot down" when Blackmore offered for her. A good girl, "despite her little ways." No wonder she took such scant interest in keeping Appleby Court up when she would soon be leaving it to go to her husband's home. But then why were the carpets and window hangings on the list? Luten would not expect his bride to refurbish his elegant residences.

And it still didn't explain her disappearance. She obviously had not run off with any man other than her intended when she was arranging her trousseau, and her intended must be either some local lad or Luten. If not Luten, then either Blackmore or Soames. She had rejected Blackmore. Stockwell thought she had had an understanding with Soames. The carpets and window hangings might have been destined for Oakhurst. There was no way to know when they had been purchased. Soames was said to be short in the pockets. She might have been planning renovations to Oakhurst.

There was not much else to be learned here in any case. When Corinne went below, she learned that Sir Reginald Prance had arrived.

Chapter Eight

She found Prance alone in the saloon, staring out the window, as elegant as ever after his trip.

"There you are!" he exclaimed when he heard her approach. "I felt as welcome as a bailiff with a lien on the furniture—no one here to greet me. What the deuce is going on, Corinne? That Friday-faced butler said Luten and Otto had gone to East Grinstead. No sign of Pattle or you. What is being done to find Susan?"

"Luten and Marchbank are arranging the ransom money."

"Then a demand has been made?" he asked eagerly.

"No, but just in case, you know. Coffen has gone to report the highwayman and—"

"You were held up *again*?" Prance's eyes opened in excitement. He clapped his white hand to his heart. "Dear girl, don't throw these alarming statements at me. Were you hurt? Did you lose much money?"

She gave him a brief description of the incident.

"I warned Pattle. But there, it is beneath me to say, 'I told you so.' I always avoid the cliché. You were not molested, and as for the rest—well, it is only money."

"Did you have a safe trip?"

"Utterly boring. I have missed all the fun!" He pouted and demanded an account of what was being done to find Susan.

She brought him up-to-date on what they had discovered thus far, omitting, for some reason she did not quite understand, the letters to and from Luten, but told him about the trousseau hidden in the blanket chest.

"Well, you have all been busy, I must say—and so has little Susan. Does a girl accumulate her bridal things without a groom in mind? How does she know he likes peach, *par exemple?* Personally I despise it on any lady over fifteen. Surely a bride ought to wear white on her wedding night, providing, of course, that she is entitled to, and one assumes Susan is.

"There is still a deal to be done. We cannot sit on our thumbs while some wretch has his way with little Susan. Let us call on Blackmore. I don't trust that customer above half. It is not like him to take a refusal lying down. He has been plotting his revenge all these months and provided himself an alibi while ordering one of his henchmen to abduct Susan from the orchard."

"He will hardly tell us if he does have her," Corinne said.

"I shall know by the looks of him. I am a bit of a dab at reading faces and gestures. I have made a study of it for my work in the theater. Grab your bonnet. I have left my carriage harnessed, ready for action. We'll have her home for lunch."

This, of course, was mere braggadocio, but it was hard to sit still, and Corinne hoped she might find some little clue at Blackmore Hall, as she had spotted the blue slippers at Greenleigh.

"It is foolishly optimistic of me to ask," Prance said, "but do they set a decent table here at Appleby?"

"Far from it."

"I feared as much, from the beggar's velvet on the furnishings. A well-ordered house does not guarantee good mutton, but an ill-run one invariably serves bad food. We shall take lunch at the Rose and Thistle."

"That's a good idea. Coffen plans to do the same. I shall tell Mrs. Malboeuf."

He shook his head. "That name alone is enough to indict her."

"Shall we leave word for Luten?"

"By all means. I shall bring you both up-to-date on my party while we eat. Odd you did not inquire," he added with another moue.

"Your parties are always stunning successes, Reg. There was no need to ask."

"That blatant flattery goes a long way in assuaging my feelings, but you really should have asked. I did it all for you and Luten." He peered at her closely. "He hasn't come up to scratch?"

"No," she said curtly. "How was the party, after we left?"

"A howling success, if I may be allowed a little tootle on my own horn. Pity you had to miss it. It went on until four. I cleverly gave all the ladies a bundle of flowers to take home, to save the job of removing them after they had left. The gentlemen jumped for those hanging from the rafters. That knock-me-down fellow, Lord Ponsonby, landed on Miss Gladstone's skirt. She leapt back like a gazelle, leaving her skirts behind, petticoats and all. Some alert lady—Lady Melbourne, I believe it was— threw a shawl over her, but not before several gentlemen discovered she is knock-kneed. It was rather amusing."

Corinne lavished the necessary praise, then left the messages, got her bonnet, and they were off.

Blackmore Hall was situated at the top of a rise, halfway to East Grinstead.

"It looks the perfect illustration for a gothic novel, does it not?" Prance asked as they drove up the graveled

61

drive. "It has all the trappings: dripping elms, that age-darkened brick, those lancet windows. All that is missing is the whirling veils of fog. One should not visit a gothic heap by daylight. Except for Strawberry Hill, of course, and it is really only a folly. It is too laughably sublime to require moonlight. That would be gilding the lily—or in its case, I suppose, the strawberry."

The carriage drew to a stop at the front of the house and they alit.

"The knocker has a nice hollow sound, just as it ought," Prance said when he lifted it a moment later. "I do feel, though, that a skull would be more in keeping with the ambience than this wheat sheaf. If we are not greeted by a hag with bad teeth, wearing a black gown, I shall be greatly disappointed in Blackmore."

Prance was destined for disappointment. It was a butler in a decent dark suit who admitted them to a well-ordered house. The paneling was dim enough to please him, but there were neither cobwebs, clanking chains, nor otherworldly groans to welcome them. They were shown into a lofty saloon whose carpet was not so very worn. The windows, while not gleaming, were not so sooted as to completely obscure the view of the park beyond. The worst he could say of the sofa was that it was like sitting on a sack of old bones.

Within minutes Lord Blackmore came to greet them. Corinne was struck by the physical similarity between the two gentlemen. Both were tall, lean, and saturnine, with skin that seemed to stretch tightly over their faces, lending them a strained air. Yet whereas Prance only looked pompous, Blackmore had a harder edge. *Sinister* was not too strong a word to use. It was his gray eyes, as cold as ice crystals, that caused it.

His bow was not quite as graceful as Prance's. "Countess, Sir Reginald," he said, strolling in. "Delighted to see you. No need to ask why you have condescended to call on me, after all these years, Countess. Let me assure you I do not have Miss Enderton sequestered in the attic, nor her body concealed in a hogshead of wine in the cellar. Yes, I did offer for her last Christmas. I was ... mildly disappointed at her refusal. The Hall required a new roof, but an obliging aunt died and that took care of that. Now, what would you have to drink? I have a decent claret ... but that is a boy's drink, eh, Prance? Brandy for you and me. I think for Lady deCoventry ..." He stopped and examined her a moment. "No, you have outgrown Madeira since my last glimpse of you. Sherry, perhaps?"

"Sherry, thank you," she said.

While he poured the drinks and passed them, Corinne was busy subjecting the saloon to a thorough visual search.

Blackmore's lips twitched as he handed her the wine. "Do feel free to take a peek behind the sofa, Lady deCoventry," he said, smiling coolly. "She would not really fit in that little escritoire you have been ogling."

"I have been admiring it," she said, trying to match his sangfroid. "French, I think?"

"Italian, actually. My using the French name confused you, perhaps. I don't know the Italian word for a desk. It is Quattrocento, in any case."

"*Scrivanìa*, I believe is the word in Italian," Prance informed him. "But Quattrocento? Cinquecento, surely, Baron?" Blackmore shrugged his shoulders. "A lovely thing, in any case. *Bellissimo!*" Prance said, smiling at it. "One would not have thought it would suit so well in a Tudor saloon."

Blackmore wafted his hand around the walls. "Flemish paintings, some Italian and some French furnishings, Oriental carpets, and a good old Kent chest to anchor it

63

all. I refer, of course, to Kent the cabinetmaker, not the county."

"*Ça va sans dire,*" Prance said. "It takes a good eye to succeed with the eclectic style," he added, nodding his head in approval.

Blackmore's lips twitched in amusement. "I cannot take credit for the accumulation, but only the current arrangement," he said. "Each generation adds what it feels is best."

"Then this excellent taste must be hereditary," Prance said, with a bow of his head.

Blackmore returned the bow with a perfectly straight face, but Corinne noticed his steely eyes were laughing. "I have my heart set on upgrading the family china," he said. "A set designed with the family crest by Wedgewood, perhaps. I am working on a design."

"I should adore to see it," Prance said at once. "I do hope it will have some black in it, to honor your title. I envisage a creamy background, with black and gold—yes, definitely gold. Griffins would be nice."

"Unfortunately, the family crest features lions," Blackmore said.

"As does my own, Baron. Three lions passant, gold on sable."

"Perhaps you will give me the benefit of your experience, Sir Reginald."

"I was hoping you would ask!" Prance was so pleased, he was purring.

It was the baron's turn to bow his head. "I have more than enough furnishings. There are some quite decent pieces in the house, but scattered about the two dozen bedrooms. And believe it or not, a mural by Angelica Kauffmann in the attic, of all places."

Prance leaned so far forward he nearly fell off the sofa.

"No!" he exclaimed in rapture. "But I adore Angelica! Which period?"

"It is done in the Italian style, probably after her visit to Italy. I would love to know how it comes to be there. An affair with one of my ancestors, perhaps. You must come upstairs to see it, Sir Reginald."

He turned a mischievous eye to Corinne. "Do join us, milady. You shall have a tour of the whole house. That will give you an opportunity to peek about and assure yourself that it does not harbor any nineteenth-century heiresses."

"Oh, I say!" Prance exclaimed, laughing. "Were we that obvious?"

"Like a pane of glass, Sir Reginald. Speaking of glass . . ."

He put one hand on Sir Reginald's elbow, the other on Lady deCoventry's, and led them forth.

Corinne said, when they left an hour later, "I have been given tours before, but that is the strangest visit I ever made! Imagine him opening every chest and making us look into the clothespresses and under the beds."

"A marvelous collection. A veritable treasure trove. There is nothing like it outside a royal palace. Prinny would be green with envy if he could see it. Well, we know one thing. The baron doesn't have Susan. I must say, I liked the chap. I had no idea he was so cultured. To hear the locals talk, one would take him for the original Wicked Baron."

"He's smooth, all right."

"Delightful! Perfectly delightful. We need not worry that he had anything to do with Susan's abduction. He's a gentleman of refinement. Susan is adorable, but there is no denying her charms are rustic. She wears such modest little gowns. Mind you, I've never seen a finer clavicle! But can you see her in that marvelous French bed in the master bedchamber? I cannot! It would take a du Barry to do it justice."

Reacting from the nervous tension of the visit, Corinne fell into a fit of the giggles. "Sorry, Reg. I fear I'm having the vapors. It was all so strange."

"Well, have them quickly. We must get on to the inn. Civilized conversation awakens other appetites. Now, don't frown, *cara mia*. I am referring to lunch. We shall eat—no, dine. On such a fine day it ought to be *al fresco*."

Chapter Nine

By daylight, East Grinstead was seen to be a pleasant little town with a wide High Street lined with shops and picturesque houses built of timber. Corinne recognized a few of the locals on the street from her former visit and greeted them. Knowing her connection to Susan, they commiserated with her on Susan's disappearance. None of them had any information to help find her.

The proprietor of the Rose and Thistle directed Sir Reginald and Lady deCoventry to a private parlor where Luten and Coffen were having a glass of ale while waiting for them. Corinne thought the inn a shabby place, but Prance, who delighted in anything antique and authentic, was enchanted with it. Its termite-ridden wainscoting ran halfway up the wall, where it met smoke-laden stucco and beamed oak. On the groaning sideboard, the dented pewter plates and tankards from the Tudor period lent the proper touch of Olde England. All that was lacking was a wild boar roasting on the spit and sawdust on the floor. At least the proprietor had not tampered with authenticity by covering the discolored old floor planks with a new-fangled oilcloth covering.

Luten was never happy to see Corinne with Prance, who played at being her flirt. "Where the devil have you been?" he demanded when they entered.

Corinne ignored him. It was Prance who replied, "Is

that any way to greet a poor traveler? Naturally we have been looking for Susan."

They sat down and summoned a servant. It was well known that Prance couldn't order a glass of water without wanting to know its pedigree. After a prolonged discussion, he ordered a steak and kidney pudding to go with the setting, and Corinne asked for chicken.

When they had all been served, Luten demanded what they had learned. "I assume you would have mentioned it if you had found her," he said.

"Our luck was not so stunning as that, which is not to say our time was wasted," Prance replied, picking at his pie with the tip of his fork. He was a finicky eater. "We can tell you for a certainty that Blackmore does not have Susan. By a process of elimination we must eventually discover who does."

"If we are to eliminate the more than ten million inhabitants of the island who do not have her, she will die of old age before we find her. More to the point, did you search Blackmore Hall?" Luten asked, thinking he was delivering a leveler.

"As a matter of fact, we did," Corinne told him. "Blackmore quite insisted on it. He showed us over the whole house." To repay Luten for his surly mood, she added, "He is much nicer than I ever imagined. Really very distinguished. I cannot think why he is spoken of so badly."

"The place is a veritable treasure trove!" Prance exclaimed. "A mural by Angelica in the attic, Luten. Imagine!"

"Angelica who?" Coffen asked.

"Wipe your mouth—with your napkin!" Prance ordered. "Angelica Kauffmann, naturally. Do you know any other artists named Angelica?"

"Can't say I do, including Kauffmann. A kraut-eater, is she?"

"God forgive him, for he knows not what he says. The lady was Swiss-born. That disadvantage was overcome by travel—Italy, naturally, then England. She was a member of the Royal Academy—quite an accomplishment for a lady. But enough art history. Blackmore Hall is stuffed to overflowing with objets d'art. If the baron needed blunt, he would have only to take some of his paintings to London." He ticked off half a dozen of the artists in the collection.

"He sounds an acquisitive gentleman," Luten said. "It is well known that collectors will sink to any ruse when they wish to acquire—"

Prance just shook his head. "She is not there, Luten. He even insisted on moving a longcase clock and showing us the priest's hole."

"Did you also examine the cellar?"

"Certainly we did. And an excellent cellar he has laid down, too. I tell you she is not there. He was perfectly at ease, even playful."

"It sounds an odd sort of call, showing you every nook and cranny. Almost as if he were trying to prove something. He would hardly keep her at his own house if he had abducted her," was Luten's next try. "She might be in the barn—or even buried nearby."

"If he buried her, then he would not get her blunt," Corinne pointed out. "One would assume he kidnapped her to force her into marriage. Odd that a man like Blackmore would have to force a lady. . . ."

"Inconceivable," Prance decreed. "If he would only grace London with his presence, he would be overwhelmed with heiresses."

Luten was becoming more vexed by the moment. His real annoyance was that Corinne had spent the time with

Prance. She had also praised Blackmore, and her gleaming eyes expressed tacit approval of Prance's knowledge of art. She had hardly glanced at Luten himself since entering.

"I see our success has put you in a pelter, Luten," Prance said. "I shall put the smile back on your face by my report on my party—for which you did not think to inquire, though it was thrown in your honor."

"Surely in honor of solving the mystery of Corinne's stolen pearls," Luten said. A light flush rose up from his collar at the mention of that party, and the tacit reminder of his not having come up to scratch.

While Prance lavished praise on his party, Luten listened impatiently, then immediately reverted to the search for Susan. "You are convinced, on very little evidence, that Blackmore is innocent. I feel equally strongly that Otto is innocent."

"Surely there was no question of Otto Marchbank having kidnapped her?" Prance asked.

"He was in charge of her monies. I had thought he might have managed to lose it and be using this ploy to account for the loss. Pretend he had paid the kidnapper, I mean, and actually paid his debts. I saw the Consols with my own eyes. He has not only got every penny of the twenty-five thousand but has managed to add ten thousand to it over the years."

"Egads! I must pick his brains before we leave. My own investment agent is hopeless. So she is now worth thirty-five thousand!" Prance exclaimed. "A veritable heiress!"

"You had only to see Marchbank's distress to know he is innocent," Corinne said.

Coffen stopped eating long enough to have his say. "We ain't much closer to finding her, despite our work.

Prance says Blackmore is innocent; you, Luten, say Otto is not to blame. Who is left?"

"Rufus Stockwell," Luten replied. Corinne made a pooh-poohing sound. "Or Jeremy Soames," he added. "Soames is next on our list."

"Surely you are omitting the likeliest suspect—a chance passerby, smitten by her beauty. A stranger, in other words," Prance pointed out. "We have known Jeremy forever. He is her cousin. He likes Susan. If he needed blunt, he would be more likely to turn highwayman than to harm her."

Coffen frowned into his ale, then looked a question at Corinne. "You don't figure it was Jeremy who held us up last night? The constable suspects a local lad. There's been a rash of thefts in Ashdown Forest and the road north of it."

Corinne gave a *tsk* of impatience. "He could use the money, but I don't see him as a highwayman. It's interesting that he had a falling out with Susan when she refused his offer. Revenge is sweet." She looked around for the others' views.

Luten shook his head and said, "Bah."

"We should talk to him," she persisted. "And if he proves innocent, then we must have broadsheets printed and post a reward for her safe return. Someone must have seen her being taken away. The roads would have been full of people on fair day."

"I quizzed Hodden," Coffen said. "No one saw hide nor hair of her, but there were dozens of carts and carriages on the road. She might have been hidden under a load of manure."

Prance gave him a scathing look and frowned at his pie.

"If it was a kidnapping, why hasn't there been a ransom note?" Luten asked.

71

Corinne sighed. "I wonder if wolves have not come back to the island and eaten her."

Prance sighed and pushed away his plate. "I wish you would keep a civil tongue in your heads," he said.

"Who will call on Jeremy?" Corinne asked. "We need not all go."

"I'll go," Luten said.

"I'll have a look around any empty barns or buildings in the neighborhood," Coffen decided. "No need to wait until dark for that. Someone might have stashed her in an empty building. No more unlikely than what the rest of you are saying anyhow. Eaten by wolves. Rubbish."

Prance patted his arm. "You must not take those little flights of fancy too literally, Pattle."

"I never take you literally," Coffen said, then frowned, wondering what that meant. "Anyhow, I'm going to find Susan."

"Where?" Prance asked, with mild interest.

"Wherever she's at."

Corinne called them to order. "I think we should go back to Appleby first, just to make sure no ransom note has come during our absence."

Luten rose. "Oakhurst is along the way. I'll stop and speak to Soames." He looked at Corinne to see if she cared to join him.

Instinct urged her to accept, as she did want to talk to Soames and ascertain exactly the nature of his romance with Susan and, most important, the reason for its rupture. But she was in no mood to oblige Luten. "I'll go home with Reggie. Are you ready to leave, Reg?" she asked.

He had begun a sketch of the parlor. "I thought this might make an interesting domestic study, suitable for framing in the kitchen. I see no reason why the servants should be robbed of art. It has a benign influence on character. André, my chef, keeps a marble statuette that he claims is a likeness of Lucullus on the windowsill for inspiration." He glanced up from his sketching and said to Corinne, "I shan't be a moment, *cara mia*. Don't let us keep you, Luten." He directed a small, triumphant smile at his friendly foe.

Luten was obliged to ignore it. It was unthinkable to give Corinne the idea he was disappointed. "Very well. I'll see you back at Appleby, then."

When Corinne and Prance returned to Appleby, they discovered that no ransom note had arrived during their absence. Otto had obviously been drinking steadily during the day but was still able to stand and speak. After his usual question, "Have you learned anything?" and the unsatisfactory answer, he retired to his study.

"For lack of anything better to do, let us go riding through the fields and woods on the off chance of finding some trace of her," Prance suggested. "It will keep our minds occupied. We don't all want to end up drunk, like Otto. I feel for him in his grief. It is a great error for a man not to have some creative outlets. I do not count making money as a creative outlet. That is mere ciphering."

Corinne suggested they wait until Luten returned, so they might learn what Soames had said.

"Meanwhile you can put on your habit and be ready to leave," Prance suggested.

"Oh dear! I didn't bring mine with me. I packed in a hurry."

"Won't Susan's fit you? She wouldn't mind."

"It will be a little short, but that is no matter. I'll do it."

Chapter Ten

When she came down, Luten had brought Jeremy Soames back to Appleby with him. Coffen had spotted them. Upon learning that a search of any abandoned buildings had already been made, he returned to Appleby with them.

Soames was a pleasant young man, with "gentleman farmer" written all over him. Fresh air, plenty of riding, and good country mutton had given him a ruddy complexion and a fine physique. He was considered a dashing buck in East Grinstead, but beside his London friends, the edge of rusticity was apparent. His jacket, while of good blue worsted, bulged where it should sit flat. The dotted Belcher kerchief he wore in lieu of a cravat suggested a streak of dandyism. His top boots lacked the smooth finish of Hoby's, the cobbler favored by the ton. His chestnut hair, cut by a local barber, showed the rough edges of country barbering. He spoke in a voice just a little too loud for ears accustomed to polite saloons. It was his eyes, however, that betrayed a certain lack of innocence. They were light green, almost yellow.

"I am so glad you have all come to help us," he said, after greeting the group. "I have been trying to put a rocket under old Otto, but he is usually in his cups, you know. A good deal worse than usual since Susan's disappearance."

"Have you any idea what might have happened to her?" Corinne asked.

"My favorite suspect is Blackmore," he said. "The man has no character. You have only to speak to him to see what he is."

Prance mounted his high horse. "I found him particularly gentlemanly. So cultured for the provinces."

"If you're talking about his pictures and whatnot, I would like to know where he is getting the blunt for them."

"They were inherited. Any new acquisitions were bought with the money from an inheritance from his aunt in Scotland, I believe," Prance replied stiffly.

"And the uncle in Cornwall. Convenient how all his relatives live so far away," Soames said. "It seems to me he's buried more relatives than he ever mentioned having."

"His mama was a Fowey, I believe. An old Cornwall family," Prance said. "The death of two relatives in a year hardly seems excessive to me. I lost twice that many last year. Unfortunately for me, their passing did not enrich my coffers."

"Your cousin Bertie left you his hounds," Coffen reminded him.

"In spite, since I used to complain of their racket."

"They enriched your coffers, though. You sold 'em to me for a pretty steep price."

"A bargain, Pattle. But this has nothing to do with Susan. *Revenons à nos moutons*."

"Well, p'raps it wasn't Blackmore," Soames said, frowning. "I wouldn't put it a pace past Rufus Stockwell. I've seen him ogling Susan in church when he thinks no one is watching him. And she giving him every encouragement, too. Susan has changed lately."

"What do you mean, changed?" Corinne asked.

75

"I daresay all I mean is that she is growing up."

"One would not guess it to look at this place," Prance said, glancing around. "Appleby has gone to rack and ruin. But perhaps we can blame Otto for that."

"That is not quite fair, Sir Reginald," Soames said. "The estate is well enough run. If it were mine, I would tile that back fifty acres and upgrade the stock. The corn yield is not what it could be either, but it is not exactly mismanaged. It is the house that is falling apart. One should not speak ill of her now, but that is Susan's doing, I fear."

Luten's gray eyes focused on Soames's face a moment. He opened his lips to speak, then closed them again.

"Why did she let things go so badly?" Corinne asked.

Soames threw up his hands. They were strong, capable hands accustomed to holding reins and wielding hammers, to birthing a calf or breaking in a horse. Hands, she thought, that could easily overpower a lady.

"I don't know. When I asked her—hinted at it discreetly, you know—she gave a sly look and intimated she would not be here long. It encouraged me to hope she might accept an offer from me. She drove out with me half a dozen times, led me on really, but in the end she refused. I thought it must be one of you she had in her eye," he said, looking first at Luten, then Prance, and finally, without much interest, at Coffen.

"I am bound to say such a thing never entered my head," Prance said. "Much as I like Susan, she is not quite my idea of a wife."

"I would have her in a minute," Coffen said, "but I didn't bother to offer. I knew she would turn me down flat. A man knows."

Luten did not commit himself on the matter.

Corinne said, "There was no one locally, then, who might fill the bill?"

"She wasn't seeing anyone hereabouts," Soames said. "And she didn't visit anyone outside the parish, other than yourself, Lady deCoventry."

"She hadn't been to London in a year," Corinne said.

Soames nodded. "It was early this spring that she mentioned not being here at Appleby for long. I would have heard if any local lad was courting her. She is quite the belle of the parish. Before that, she had spoken of hiring a new housekeeper. Malboeuf is hopeless, of course. Susan was speaking at the time of refurbishing the place."

"What did she plan to do?" Corinne asked. "New window hangings, I expect? A new carpet—perhaps a chaise longue?"

"I don't recall exactly. The carpets are not actually that worn. It is just that they have not been lifted and beaten in years. The window frames are covered in mildew. The frames have to be repaired. And of course, the panes are coated in dust. It is a shame to let a fine house like this fall into such a state when a hundred pounds would put it shipshape."

"What about Stockwell?" Luten asked. "Might Susan have had him in her eye?"

Soames looked astonished. "Rufus? Good lord, she wouldn't be interested in him. I doubt he clears five hundred a year from Greenleigh. He is a nice enough fellow. He sold me a milcher at a good price, but she would not marry him. No, I feel our man is Blackmore. There is nothing he would stick at. She turned him down, his pride was wounded, and he has chosen this revenge."

"That was my own feeling," Luten said.

"*Et tu*, Luten?" Prance said. "Pray remember we are speaking of a gentleman."

"Aye, he tries to give that impression," Soames said. "He wears a fancy jacket and stares down his nose at a fellow. I don't visit the man. I wouldn't darken his door if you paid me. I have some ideas where his wealth is coming from. But I shall say no more on that score or he'll have me up for slander."

Coffen said apologetically, "Don't mean to cut into your gossip, Soames, but have you any evidence he took off Susan?"

"I'm sure the bounder has her. I have been keeping a sharp eye on him in any case." He drew out a clumsy turnip watch and glanced at it. "Good Lord, I'm late. I am supposed to be at an auction at Wetherby's place this minute, and it is five miles away. Wetherby is selling up and retiring. There ought to be some bargains on the block. I could use a new pair of plow horses. A shocking price they are asking for them."

Tobin appeared at the door, removing a half apron as he came, and accompanied Mr. Soames out. "Let me know at once if you learn anything," Soames called, before leaving.

Luten looked at the others. "What did you make of him?" he asked.

"He talked a lot about money," Coffen said.

"I don't believe that indicates a mercenary nature so much as a lack of funds," Prance said. "Soames is esurient. He has just enough to know he needs more to be fully accepted in the best society. An ambitious lad, I would say. He didn't waste a minute when he thought Susan was interested. He's even done a tally to figure out the cost of repairs to the place."

Corinne said, "You're right, Reg. Soames is a climber. He wanted Susan to hire a house in London. He was upset when Susan jilted him, too. You notice he was swift to accuse Blackmore."

"He made some curious statements about Blackmore," Luten said. "Was he implying the sudden wealth came from gambling? One thing is clear. Soames suspects Blackmore. Soames is awake on all suits. He has been here, to see how things were going on. If he suspects Blackmore, then it reinforces my intention to have a thorough search of his outbuildings after dark. At least if Blackmore has her, she isn't dead. He would have to marry her to get his hands on her fortune."

"True," Prance said. "Shall we go for that ride now, Corinne?" He turned to Luten. "Before you chide us for slacking off, Luten, let me assure you that we mean to search the woods and meadows for Susan, or any sign of her passing by. I shall just have a word with my man before leaving. He was to find me a decent bedchamber and air the bed." He left.

Luten accompanied Corinne to the hall to wait for Prance. "I see you are back in short skirts, Countess," he said, looking askance at her borrowed riding habit. When she pokered up, he smiled to show her he was jesting. "Should you not let your hair down, to complete the effect of girlish charm? Very becoming, despite your years." He reached out and flicked a loose curl. "I understand it is the custom in Ireland for gentlemen to marry late. It must be a sad trial to the ladies, having to go on feigning youth into their declining years."

"I wouldn't know, Luten. I, unlike the other ladies, was snatched from the cradle. Now, if you have released your ill humor, I have something I would like to say to you."

"That will be a pleasant change. One is hard-pressed to get a word in edgewise when Prance is in the room."

"I was mistaken. You are *not* over your little fit of jealousy."

His delicate eyebrows rose an inch. "Jealousy?"

"At Prance's doing all the talking. Whatever did you think I meant?" she asked, with an arch smile.

"What was it you wanted to say?"

"I saw Susan's trousseau. Why did you not tell me about it?"

"I made sure you would discover it, in your own good time. You think it was a trousseau, then?"

"A lady does not put up with the slithery, cold feel of a silk nightgown for her own pleasure. They are horrid."

"You were accustomed to a good warm flannelette nightie in Ireland, I expect?"

"Oh no, we didn't have special nightwear. We just huddled in front of the peat grate in our daytime rags, fighting with the dog over the family bone." Having given him a setdown, she continued. "I also found some interesting lists."

"Of possible suitors to admire the silk nightie?"

"No, of things to buy, I think. One was for lingerie, the other for window hangings, carpet, a chaise longue."

"So that is what put the notion of a chaise longue in your head! I thought you must have been reading a French novel. A trousseau and a shopping list of items for her new home, then? Is that your meaning?"

"Yes. Strange, is it not? Added to what she intimated to Soames, it seems as if she was thinking of getting married, yet there is no indication who the groom could be." She waited, thinking Luten might mention that he had been corresponding with Susan recently.

"Whoever he is, he will be disappointed if we don't find her," he said.

Prance came downstairs. "You would not believe the state of the linen in this house. You can see through it, it is so worn. I say, you're not coming with us, Luten?"

"No, I told you, I plan to ride over Blackmore's land."

"Without permission?" Prance asked.

"Without permission. If he objects, that will be an indication that he has something to hide."

Coffen came ambling out and overheard him. "I might as well go with you, Luten," he said. "No point sitting here looking at my boots."

Prance glanced at his boots. "No, you would be better employed polishing them. Shall we go, my sweet?" He offered Corinne his arm.

"*Au revoir,* angel of delight," Luten said, with a satirical grin and an exaggerated bow.

She waved good-bye and left with Prance.

Chapter Eleven

When Corinne returned from her ride with Prance and went to Susan's bedchamber to change out of her riding habit, she found a pair of clean sheets sitting on the bed. Luten had mentioned having his valet get sheets at the inn. Knowing the shortage of help at Appleby, she decided to change the linen herself. It took her back to her days in Ireland, when she and her sister Kate had performed these light chores together. She was not aware of the nostalgic smile that played on her lips as she began her job.

Luten noticed it when he came to the door a little later. He observed her a moment, with a strange twisting feeling in his chest, before tapping lightly and stepping in.

"Oh, Luten. Thank you for the sheets," she said.

"You don't have to make the bed yourself," he replied. "My servants will see to it."

"Let them cook instead. I'm quite capable of making a bed."

She found the job awkward without Kate to help her, though. Luten watched for a moment, then went to the opposite side of the bed and began tugging at the sheet to straighten it out.

"Did Blackmore order you off his land?" she asked, tucking in a corner.

"I didn't see him. I spoke with his game warden. The

man made a point of telling me Blackmore was at the fair the day Susan vanished and entertained company that evening. Did you and Prance have any luck?"

"You have to tuck the sheet under the mattress, Luten, or my feet will stick out tonight and be cold." He began shoving the corners in. "We met a couple of schoolboys, fishing for tadpoles in the pond. They said the Wicked Baron had got her. In fact, they said they saw her in his saloon last night."

Luten dropped the sheet. "I knew it! Where are they? We must—"

"It is all a hum, Luten. They said she was sitting on Blackmore's knee, kissing him, and he gave her some money. Gold coins. *She* was kissing *him*. That's what they said."

"There might be something in it, if he fed her brandy," Luten said, and began work again.

"Well, if there is, Susan had dyed her hair. The lady who was kissing Blackmore was a dasher with black hair."

"Don't they know Susan has blond hair?"

"Apparently not. They are too young to be enamored of her," she said, examining him closely. His pensive face revealed nothing. "Since he was paying the woman, it suggests she was nothing else but a light-skirt."

"A gentleman doesn't entertain a light-skirt in his own home."

"Well, he is a bachelor." She picked up the top sheet and shook it out. It seemed strange to be doing this sort of menial work again and positively unreal to be doing it with Luten. Yet he did a good job of it. Better than she. His emerald ring flashed as he reached out and caught the corner of the sheet and pulled it taut. He had lovely hands, with long, artistic fingers.

"I think the lads were just making up stories," she said.

"Blackmore does have a reputation for liking women," he replied. "No doubt you noticed it?"

"Since he was equally charming to Reggie, I assumed it was just his normal manner. The lads I spoke of asked Reggie what their information was worth. It's odd, though, that they insisted the lady had black hair."

"What does Prance think?"

"He thinks it is all a hum."

Luten picked up the blanket and tossed it on the bed.

"I don't need that," she said. "It was warm in bed last night. Just the counterpane."

When the silk sheet had been put on top, Luten unceremoniously kicked the soiled linen into the hallway. "There! We have made your bed, now w—you must lie in it."

He looked a little self-conscious at his near slip. Unlike Luten to come so close to a solecism. "We have made Susan's bed. How foolish! We should have made up a different one. I only slept here last night because the others had no linen."

"It is no matter. When we get her back, we'll make up another one for you."

She gazed at him a moment. "We will get her back, won't we, Luten?" she asked uncertainly. When she felt her bottom lip begin to wobble, she caught it between her teeth in a gesture that always made Luten want to kiss away her fears.

"There is no reason to think otherwise," he said gruffly.

"I wonder if she was in some sort of trouble. She didn't say anything to you? Write anything, I mean?" She waited, hoping he would tell her what was in those letters they had exchanged recently.

"Enceinte, you mean?" he asked.

"I suppose that is the first thing that comes to mind

when we speak of an unmarried girl being in trouble, but I didn't mean that, necessarily."

After a frowning pause, he said, "If she was, she didn't confide in me. I wish to God she had."

"Where would she go, if that is why she ran away?"

"I expect she'd leave the parish. Go somewhere that she's unknown until she had delivered the child and made some arrangements for its upbringing."

"I hate to think of her being alone. I wish she had written to me. Surely she would have, if—"

"Don't torture yourself with these useless imaginings, my dear," Luten said gently. When he took her hand and squeezed her fingers, she had to blink away the tears. "She wouldn't just run off with no money, or very little, and without her clothing. She would have invented a visit to a relative and gone in her own carriage. Susan isn't a fool."

"Still, I can't help feeling guilty. I haven't written to her for a month. I should have kept a closer eye on her."

"She wasn't your responsibility. She is no real blood kin to you. She was George's cousin—and mine. If anyone should feel guilty, it's I."

"We must find her, and when we do, I plan to make it up to her."

"I know how you feel. I feel the same," Luten said, then shook his head wearily. "You'd best change for dinner."

When she had changed into her rose evening gown and gone out her door, she noticed the soiled linen had been removed. Luten must have taken it away. Probably just kicked it down the kitchen stairs. He had been very sweet, helping her with the bed. But he hadn't revealed what he and Susan had been corresponding about.

Belowstairs, Corinne discovered the others had already gone to the dining room. She hurried in after them.

85

"Don't blame me if the mutton is dry as a bone," Mrs. Malboeuf said, slapping a nearly raw joint of beef in front of Mr. Marchbank. She wore a clean apron and had her hair tucked neatly under her cap. Marchbank picked up the carving knife, but his dazed eyes could hardly focus.

"Let me do that for you, Otto," Luten said, and carried the platter to the other end of the table himself, as Tobin was busy at the sideboard arranging vegetables.

"Try to find a piece that is at least warm for me," Prance said, with a worried eye at the puddle of blood gathering in the plate. Meat of any sort was his least favorite food. He felt like a cannibal when it was rare.

"I shall just have vegetables tonight," Corinne said.

"There was a bit of ham in the larder," Tobin told her, handing her a plate of ham sliced paper-thin to cover the plate.

Coffen had no objection to raw beef, but said a bit of Yorkshire pudding would have been nice.

"I only have two hands, haven't I?" Mrs. Malboeuf barked, in a voice more usually heard in a kennel.

"What happened to that footman you were going to send to the kitchen, Luten?" Corinne asked, when Mrs. Malboeuf had departed.

"I decided he would be better employed in looking for Susan. It won't kill us to fast for a few days. He has been out searching the fields and ditches and questioning the neighbors. He learned nothing new."

Prance related what the boys had told him about Blackmore entertaining a black-haired lady. When Coffen mentioned that he hadn't likely kidnapped Susan if he already had a lady on kissing terms, Luten decided their story was a hum.

The meal was nearly inedible, but at least there was not much of it. No soup, no fish course. Only the mutton, potatoes, carrots, and a runny syllabub for dessert. By the time the syllabub was finished, Otto's head had sunk to his chest. Snoring sounds issued from his lips. The gentlemen carried him to the sofa in his study. When they returned to the dining room, they were too late to take port. Mrs. Malboeuf was already there. The plates had not been cleared, but she was making a great production of sweeping the floor.

"If you're looking for her ladyship, she's in the saloon," she told them.

"A mouse, let alone a man, could die of thirst in this house, if he didn't starve to death first," Coffen said. He took the tray holding glasses and a bottle of port from the sideboard, and they went to the saloon, where Corinne sat on a footstool, alone, before the cold grate.

"What a delightful scene!" Prance exclaimed. "Like something out of a melodrama. Patience on a footstool, smiling at ashes."

"She ain't smiling," Coffen said. "Nothing to smile at."

"That dinner was nearly as strange as our visit to Blackmore, Prance," she said, with a wan smile, which did not prevent her from seeing Luten's scowl out of the corner of her eye.

"You are kind to call that meal strange. It was barbaric! Tomorrow we shall take dinner as well as lunch at the Rose and Thistle," Prance said, patting her hand and drawing her to a sofa. "We don't want our little Irish Rose to sink into a decline. I have been looking forward to seeing you in that gorgeous rose silk gown. *Formidable!*" he said, giving the word a French twist.

Luten gave a huff of disgust. "A cold, slithery gown for our delight, Countess?" he asked. "What a deal of discomfort you ladies put up with to amuse us."

"Don't pay him any heed," Corinne said to Prance.

"I never do, my sweet. How should I pay heed to

anyone or anything else when I am by your side, basking in your radiance?"

"You'd ought to be paying some heed to poor Susan." Coffen scowled. "As soon as I've had a gargle, I mean to ride around the neighborhood. Luten plans to search Blackmore's place. What are you going to do, Reg?"

"Don't worry about me. I can amuse myself."

"I ain't worried about you. I'm worried about Susan."

"I shall drive into East Grinstead and engage the locals in gossip, see what I can pick up."

"Go and sit yourself in a snug tavern, having a few wets, you mean," Coffen said accusingly.

"Actually, that's not a bad idea," Luten said. One part of the idea's charm was that it got him away from Corinne. "I'll mention the broadsheets and the reward to Otto, if he's sobered up yet. What sum do you think we should offer?"

"We?" Prance asked. "Surely the reward will come out of Susan's money. How does one word it—'Reward for any information leading to her discovery'? And a description, of course. Blond hair, blue eyes, five foot three inches."

"Four inches. And she was wearing a blue mulled muslin dress," Coffen said. His blue eyes stared into the distance.

Prance got a pen and paper, and they wrote up the notice while they had their port. Shadows were lengthening by the time they had agreed on the details. They were about to leave when the door knocker sounded. They all gave a start of alarm.

"The ransom note!" Coffen cried, and went pelting to the door.

Tobin beat him to it. It was Jeremy Soames who had come to call. He still wore his blue jacket and top boots.

He made a rustic bow and said, "Pardon my outfit. I

88

decided to stop on my way back from the auction. Any news?"

"Did you get your horses?" Coffen asked.

"I did. And a dandy farm cart as well. It will come in handy for moving manure and marl about the fields. So you've heard nothing about Susan?"

"No, nothing," Luten said.

Soames looked around the room, then went to sit beside Corinne on the sofa. "This must be very trying for you, Lady deCoventry," he said. "You and Susan were such good friends. She often spoke of you."

"We are all very worried," she said.

"You mustn't let it get you down. Why don't I take you for a hurl in my carriage tomorrow? Or better, come to me for tea. You must be starved here. Mrs. Malboeuf is a wretched cook."

Mr. Soames's greenish eyes glinted hopefully. Corinne realized that he was trying to court her. Her fortune didn't match Susan's, but she had a small country property, a house on Berkeley Square, and a competence. No doubt she seemed rich to him.

"I would rather not commit myself, Mr. Soames," she said. "I want to be free, in case anything comes up, you know."

"Dash it, why don't you call me Jeremy? We have known each other for years, on and off."

"Thank you, Jeremy. Perhaps another time."

He seemed satisfied with his progress. "I am off, then. I have a little something I mean to check up on tonight. I shall be in touch tomorrow. Think about my offer. My housekeeper is an excellent cook."

This speech revealed his standing. A gentleman's housekeeper was not expected to cook as well.

After he left, Coffen said, "He's got his eye on you, Corinne, now that he's lost Susan."

"A man's reach must exceed his grasp or what's an heiress for?" Prance said airily.

"I'm hardly an heiress," Corinne said.

Coffen fell into a heavy frown. "That *kooie bono* you mentioned once, Prance—"

"*Cui bono?* Who profits? Now, there is an idea, Pattle! Who inherits Appleby and the money if Susan—God forbid—should turn up dead?"

"That's what I'm trying to say," Coffen said. "Soames inherits. That's who. Susan's papa and his were not only cousins but close friends. Of course, it wasn't likely that Susan would die before Jeremy, but Jeremy was to get the lot if Susan died before she married. And Susan was to get Oakhurst if Jeremy cocked up his toes."

"Now, isn't that interesting!" Prance said.

Luten detached himself from the chimneypiece where he was lounging and came to attention. "He said he was going to check up on something."

"Going to see that no one's found Susan, the bounder," Coffen said, legging it toward the door. "I'm after him."

"Go with him," Luten said to Prance.

"In my second best evening jacket? Oh, very well. But I shall demand that Susan replace it if it's destroyed." He darted out after Coffen.

"Perhaps you should go with them," Corinne said to Luten.

"The two of them can handle Soames. I still want to make a search of Blackmore's outbuildings."

He also hurried out, leaving her alone. With a long evening of waiting stretching in front of her, she hopped up and asked Tobin to have Susan's mount sent around with Coffen's and Prance's, then darted upstairs for her pelisse. She would follow Soames with Coffen and Prance—and make a great mess of her good rose gown,

90

but it couldn't be helped. She could not face the evening alone in this inhospitable house with the cold grate.

She felt that they were finally on the right track. Soames had offered for Susan, she had tumbled to his mercenary nature and jilted him; he had taken his revenge by trying to force her into marriage. And if that failed, he still got her money by killing her. . . . Had he already done it? Pray God they were not too late!

Chapter Twelve

Appleby was dim and gloomy, but when Corinne left it, she felt she had stepped into a dark tunnel. A tattered rag of cloud hid the waxing moon. A scattering of stars twinkling bravely in the black velvet sky was pretty but gave poor light. The fresh air was welcome, however. A warm breeze carried the spring scents of blossoms and grass and earth.

As her eyes adjusted to the darkness, she spotted Coffen and Prance, waiting for their mounts, and darted forward to join them. The mounts were brought around, and Prance gave her a lift into the saddle of Susan's gray cob, Dancer. Prance had brought his mount with him. Coffen rode the aging hack that was kept for Otto but seldom ridden. The three rode down the pebbled drive to the main road.

"Luten won't like it, your coming with us," Coffen said to Corinne, with very little hope of deterring her.

"He won't know. He's gone to Blackmore's by the back way. We leave by the main road."

"In theory, I am against your coming," Prance said. "But welcome to the chase, *cara mia*. Did anyone happen to notice which way Soames went?"

Coffen said, "I caught a glimpse of him through the trees. He turned right into the park. He's either taking a shortcut home or he's up to something. Ride carefully.

He'll hear three horses creeping up behind him. Why don't you go along to the tavern by the main road as you planned, Reg? If he outwits me, you might pick up the trail and follow him."

"Very well, but you must defend me if Luten cuts up stiff."

"Don't know who put him in charge anyhow," Coffen muttered. A mutiny occasionally broke out in the ranks of the Berkeley Brigade, usually when Luten was not present, and usually amounting to no more than a few grumbling complaints.

"Nor do I, but you must own he considers himself our chief. You will have more need of this than I." So saying, he handed Coffen a dark lantern. "Of course, you have a pistol?" he asked. They drew their mounts to a stop.

"Of course I have," Coffen replied.

"With bullets?" Corinne asked.

"Tobin fixed me up."

"Adieu, then," Prance called. He dug his heels into the side of his showy bay mare and clattered on toward the main road, headed to East Grinstead.

Corinne and Coffen followed Soames, keeping a good distance behind him. In the shadowy night, Soames was more likely to hear them than see them. He jogged along at a canter for about a mile, obviously not in a great hurry, but not dallying either. Then he veered left behind a hedgerow.

"That hedgerow is the border between Appleby and McArthur's farm," Corinne whispered.

When they passed through an opening in the hedgerow, Soames had disappeared from view. Coffen scanned McArthur's meadow. The moon peeped out from behind the clouds. Moonlight silvered the shivering grass and limned one ancient oak in charcoal against the sky. Trees at the far end of the meadow formed a dark, hulking shadow. Willows, they looked like.

"Must be a stream there," Coffen said. "P'raps Susan has drowned. We'll check it out tomorrow in daylight."

"The whole area has been searched. There! He's heading to that building!" Corinne exclaimed softly.

"I don't see him."

She pointed. "There. He's riding along in the shadow of the willows."

"I've caught him now. Oh, there's a little house there, at the back of the meadow. It disappears against the trees."

"It's a shepherd's hut. There used to be sheep in this field when Mr. McArthur was living here."

"I mind Susan saying McArthur's house burned down. I hope Soames ain't hiding Susan in a shepherd's hut!"

"Should we follow him or wait until he leaves and investigate?"

"We'll watch a bit."

They hadn't long to wait. Soames went into the hut and came out again within a minute. He mounted his nag and galloped away, toward the main road, headed toward Oakhurst, or possibly East Grinstead.

"Now, what the deuce is he up to?" Coffen said. "Prance will pick up his trail on the road. We'd best have a peek at that hut."

They wasted no time in riding to the hut. Nestled amongst the willows stood a simple earth building with a thatched roof in a poor state of repair. They heard the ripple of a stream behind the hut.

"I'll go in first. You stand guard here," Coffen said. Coffen was an awkward, ungainly fellow, but he was as graceful in the saddle as a swan in water. He handed Corinne the dark lantern, dismounted smoothly and silently, drew out his pistol, and tiptoed to the hut. When a loud neigh came from the doorway, he leapt a foot in the air and dropped his gun.

He snatched it up and scrabbled away from the doorway on his hands and knees, expecting to hear a shot ring in his ears. When no sound came, he crept slowly back to the hut, waited a moment, then peeked in. Another whinny sounded, but he was expecting it and didn't leap or fall.

When no shot rang out, Corinne dismounted and followed him. She raised the door of the dark lantern and flashed the light around the hut. There was no one and nothing there save the horse, a saddle resting in one corner, and a mound of hay with a water bucket beside it.

"It's all right. You can come in," Coffen said over his shoulder.

She joined him. "What a beauty!" she exclaimed, examining the dark mare. She let the horse smell her hand, to establish contact. When she reached out to stroke the velvet nose, the mare tossed her head and whinnied in pleasure.

"I believe this is the nag that robbed us last night, if I'm not mistaken," Coffen said, playing the lantern over the points of the mare.

"It could be the highwayman's nag," she agreed, for of course, she knew Coffen didn't mean the horse had robbed them.

"Thing to do, look for clues," he said, and began poking under the straw.

Corinne examined the saddle. "It's just an ordinary man's saddle," she said.

"Nothing here. I was hoping to find my watch."

"Here's something!" she exclaimed, and picked up a small piece of cloth that was sticking out from beneath the saddle. "It looks like a dust rag."

Coffen took it and examined it by the lantern. "By the living jingo, it's my hankie! The one Susan made me."

"The one you had your money tied up in last night?"

"The same one. I can still see the creases from the knot. We've stumbled onto the highwayman's lair. We'd best get out of here. He might come back." He tucked the handkerchief into his jacket.

"Do you think Soames is the highwayman?"

"It looks like it, or how did he know the nag was here? He was checking up on it."

"Should we tell the constable or go after him ourselves?"

"Thing to do, I believe, is tell Luten. I mean to say, it don't look as if he's planning to rob anyone tonight. He's gone home and left the nag here, so there's no rush. What I'm thinking is, if he's got Susan, then we can threaten to report him for being the highwayman if he don't give her back."

"If he has her, she's not here. Where would he keep her?"

"P'raps he's on his way to check up on her next. I'll go after him. You go back to Appleby. Tell Luten what we found, and that I've ridden after Soames, toward Oakhurst."

"Very well, but don't do anything dangerous, Coffen. If you see him go into a house or whatever, wait until he comes out, then rescue Susan."

"I'll take no chances. I'm no good to her dead."

Corinne returned to Appleby at a gallop. She was frightened, alone in the countryside at night. Tall trees growing along the roadside cast menacing shadows on the road. A breeze stirred the branches, causing a rustle that lifted the hairs on her arms. A highwayman, or a kidnapper, could be hiding behind any tree. She kicked her heels into Dancer's flanks and was home in minutes.

"Has Lord Luten returned yet?" she asked the stable-boy when she took Dancer to the stable.

"No, milady. He's only been gone less than an hour."

"Of course. No need to tell him I have been out," she said. The stableboy smirked knowingly.

She went back into the house by the front door to avoid encountering Mrs. Malboeuf. Once in the saloon, she began to think about Soames and the highwayman's mount in the hut. Just before he left, Soames had said, "I have a little something I want to check up on tonight." Perhaps he was checking up on the highwayman, looking for the place he had concealed his mount. The robber wouldn't want to leave it at a public stable in case one of his victims recognized it. There was a reward of five hundred pounds for the highwayman's capture. Soames would be happy to get that.

On the other hand, Soames hadn't been at home last night around midnight when Luten called on him, and when the highwayman had held up Coffen and her. That looked suspicious. They should ask Soames where he had been. If he had an alibi, then he wasn't the highwayman. But he might still have kidnapped Susan.

She was restless and fidgety, worried about Coffen, and as time passed, also worried about Luten. She wanted tea, but any small request was taken as a great imposition in this house. She poured a glass of wine instead and paced back and forth in the gloomy saloon. Catching a glimpse of herself in the dim mirror over the sofa, she saw her hair was all askew after her ride. She tidied it up, mindful of Luten's taunting "Lady Medusa."

Prance was the first one to return. "I saw Susan's mare in the stable. Have you lost Pattle?" he asked in alarm.

She told him the tale of the shepherd's hut. "It's been an hour now," she said. "Do you think we should go after him?"

"He should be safe. Soames was at the tavern."

"Oh, is that where he went? That doesn't look very . . . dangerous."

"Of more concern is Luten's prolonged absence. It doesn't take this long to have a peek at a few barns and a stable. If he's not back in fifteen minutes, I shall go after him."

Luten returned in ten minutes. Prance noticed that he wasn't looking quite as cocky as usual. Luten refused to look him in the eye. There was almost a tinge of sheepishness about that proud face.

"You got caught!" Prance said, and laughed in delight. "I would give a monkey to have seen that! The toplofty Marquess of Luten apologizing to Blackmore."

"One of his stableboys saw me. I was just sticking my nose into his icehouse when Blackmore himself appeared at my elbow and asked me if I'd like to borrow a lantern. He was quite gracious about it. Realized our concern for Susan, et cetera. He insisted on giving me a tour of all the buildings."

"I told you he was charming."

"What you didn't tell me is that he's a Captain Sharp."

"You played cards with him?"

"He invited me in for a glass of brandy after the guided tour. The cards were on the table. We had a few hands. Within half an hour, he had taken me for a hundred pounds."

"And you are no Johnnie Raw."

"Did he use shaved cards?" Corinne asked.

"Really!" Prance scoffed.

"They weren't shaved, but he might have marked them in some manner. If he did, I couldn't discover how he was doing it." He looked around and said, "Where's Coffen?"

"He's standing guard at Soames's place," Prance said,

and related the tale of the hut, implying without actually saying that it was he and not Corinne who had been with Coffen.

"When I went on to the tavern," Prance said, "I learned that Soames had been there for a quarter of an hour. He must have gone directly from the hut to the Rose and Thistle."

After they had discussed the possibility of Soames being the highwayman versus his trying for the reward, Luten said to Corinne, "And what have you been doing all evening, Countess?"

"Waiting," she said.

His steely gray eyes slid to her slippers, which had picked up some traces of mud in the meadow, and to the hem of her gown, which was also soiled.

"You really should have changed into that charming habit of Susan's before riding. The groom was brushing down Dancer when I returned."

She bristled, angry with herself for feeling guilty. "I decided to go with them," she said. "What's wrong with that?"

His gimlet eyes bored into her. "Why bother to lie about it if there's nothing wrong with it?" he asked. Without waiting for an answer, he turned to Prance. "Other than that slight evasion, your story is true?"

"Absolutely. My congratulations, Luten. You are awake on all suits. One can only wonder that such a sharp fellow got caught by a stableboy," he added mischievously.

"It's interesting that Blackmore has his boys on the *qui vive*. They were looking for someone."

"And found you." Prance smirked.

"Coffen wanted me to tell you what he had discovered, Luten," Corinne said. "What should we do about it?"

"As you hadn't the wits to stay at the hut and see who came for the horse, and as it apparently didn't occur to

Prance to go there when you told him you had found the highwayman's mount, then I expect I shall go now and hope it's not a case of shutting the barn door after the horse has bolted."

On that leveler, he rose and walked stiffly from the saloon.

"He can make one feel such a fool," Prance said to Corinne, then rose and went after Luten. "Shall I go with you?" he asked.

"I can manage, Prance. If you're feeling brave, you might speak to Mrs. Malboeuf about having some tea ready for our return."

"Discretion is the better part of valor. I shall transmit your message via Tobin. *He* does not bark."

Chapter Thirteen

"The whole affair was badly botched," Luten said testily. He and Coffen had returned just as Tobin carried in the tea tray. Corinne poured the tea, and they all took up a place around the grate. "You really ought to have known better, Prance. If you had gone with Coffen as you were supposed to, one of you could have stayed and watched the hut while the other followed Soames."

"Is one to assume that the horse was gone when you reached the hut?" Prance asked.

"There wasn't a sign of it."

"We know that Soames didn't take it," Corinne said. "He was in the tavern."

"I went there as soon as I saw the hut was empty," Luten said. "He wasn't there. He'd left half an hour before. Plenty of time to get to the hut and gallop off."

"And he wasn't at home either," Coffen added. "We called on him."

"Shouldn't someone be out looking for him if you think he plans to rob an innocent traveler?" Corinne asked.

"We didn't come to Appleby to catch a highwayman," Luten snapped. "We notified Hodden and suggested he send to London for a Bow Street Runner as he appears incapable of catching the fellow himself. None of this has anything to do with Susan."

"Red herring," Coffen said wisely.

"A red herring is a conscious effort to divert attention from the real matter at hand," Prance informed him. "Luten is right. The highwayman is an irrelevance. We'll leave it to Hodden."

Coffen rubbed his ear. "If it ain't Blackmore that's got Susan, and it ain't Soames, then that leaves only Stockwell."

"Or the obvious person, a stranger," Prance added.

Corinne listened to their arguments, then said, "Soames is not eliminated. If he's turned highwayman, he's obviously desperate for money. He might very well have kidnapped Susan."

"Then why hasn't he demanded a ransom?" Luten asked.

"Because he's trying to talk her into marrying him. And if she refuses, he couldn't let her go. He'd have to . . . And he is her heir, remember."

There was a short silence as her meaning sank in. Corinne noticed the pinching of Luten's nostrils. They were all worried, but he seemed to be taking it harder than the rest of them.

"We'll get a warrant and have his house searched," Luten said grimly.

Coffen scowled into his collar. "Scoundrel!"

Luten began pacing the saloon. They all knew this was his thinking mode and waited to hear what he had to say. After a few turns up and down, he stopped before the grate and said, "I don't see that we've eliminated Blackmore. Doesn't his eagerness to prove by these arranged tours that Susan is not at Blackmore Hall suggest that he has her secreted elsewhere? You know about such things, Prance. Does he own any other estates?"

"No, he doesn't even have a house in London," Prance

102

replied. "Pity. He would be a welcome addition to Society."

"He might have hired one," was Luten's next suggestion. "Or be using some abandoned house—"

"Any vacant buildings within a ten-mile radius have been searched," Corinne said. "It's Soames who has her."

Luten ignored the mention of Soames. "Then we'll search them again, and we'll broaden the radius. I shall set a twenty-four-hour watch on Blackmore as well."

"What about Soames?" Corinne asked.

"And on Soames," he agreed, but his lack of enthusiasm suggested that he thought Blackmore was the guilty party. "I'll speak to my servants at once. Simon can take the night shift. Coffen, you send your footman to keep guard on Soames's place. Follow Soames if he leaves. There's no more we can do tonight."

"We can search Soames's house," Corinne said.

"Tomorrow," Luten said impatiently. "I don't believe for a minute that Soames has Susan. Why would he have called us down to help find her if he had her himself? His house will be watched tonight, and Hodden will search it tomorrow morning to satisfy your fears, Corinne. I suggest you all get a good night's sleep."

"I shall go to my room, but I shan't retire yet," Prance said. "I've promised Blackmore a design for his new dinnerware. A few ideas are wrestling for supremacy in my cranium. I do hope they don't bring on a megrim. The layman has no idea of the mental trauma of creating."

"What do you mean, layman?" Coffen demanded. "You ain't a clergyman." Prance ignored him.

Prance rose, drew Corinne's hand to his lips for a kiss, and left. Luten exhaled a weary sigh and shook his head.

Coffen immediately reverted to his usual good-natured way. "This notion of Prance's ain't a complete waste of time, Luten. It gets him into Blackmore's house. If there's anything havey-cavey afoot, Prance will tumble to it. He's queer as Dick's hand band, but he's not stupid."

"Blackmore isn't keeping her at the Hall." His face was a mask of anguish. "Where can she be?" he murmured, really talking to himself.

Corinne's womanly compassion was touched, but despite her sympathy, she felt a twinge of jealousy. If Luten's wasn't the face of a man in love, she was much mistaken. And she still hadn't discovered the secret of those letters between Luten and Susan.

She patted his hand and said, "Try to get some sleep, Luten."

His fingers closed over hers in a crippling squeeze. "Who could sleep with this on his conscience?" he said in a distracted way. "You go on up to bed, Corinne. I know I shan't sleep. I'll stay down here awhile, thinking."

He bent down and placed a light kiss on her cheek. Luten was not prone to sentimental gestures. She thought it was a sort of vicarious kiss for Susan.

"Good night," she said, and went upstairs, wondering why he had said it was on his conscience instead of his mind. It sounded as if he held himself responsible for Susan's fate.

"Do you want me to go with you?" Coffen asked Luten when they were alone. "To Blackmore's place, I mean. I expect that's why you've stayed downstairs. Blackmore might not be so wary now that you've been caught once. Not a bad time to go."

"Thanks, Coffen, but there's less chance of being caught if I go alone. I plan to go directly to his house and peek in the windows—if he doesn't have a dog out patrolling. He didn't earlier. I wonder why he didn't." He frowned. "That's odd, don't you think? It would be more effective than having men on patrol."

"Dogs bark. Maybe that's why."

"Why should he mind that? Unless he's expecting someone whom he wants to sneak in quietly. Interesting."

"That black-haired light-skirt the lads told Prance and Corinne about?"

"I was thinking of someone more interesting. Some henchman reporting on Susan is what I mean. Well, I'm off."

"What time should I expect you back?"

"When I get here. Don't wait up."

"I'll give you an hour, then go after you," Coffen said. "It's no trouble. I'll not sleep anyway but just lie awake worrying."

Corinne was also lying awake, worrying. She didn't think Blackmore had kidnapped Susan. He seemed too carefree about the whole affair. And she didn't see why Soames hadn't sent a ransom note if he had kidnapped her, because after considering the matter, she couldn't believe he would ever kill Susan. He was ambitious but not actually evil. She thought of the trousseau, folded up in that trunk. What other secrets might the house hold? Tomorrow she'd search the spare guest rooms and the attic. Perhaps Susan had already bought the carpets and the chaise longue, too. Not that finding them would prove anything.

After a long time, her eyelids fluttered closed and she slept. She dreamt of Susan and herself, three years ago when she had spent her mourning period at Appleby Court. They were racing through the meadow, chasing rabbits and stopping to gather skirtfuls of wildflowers. It was a happy dream, but suddenly some man was chasing them through the meadow. A man who seemed familiar, but when she turned to look at him, he had no face. She

105

and Susan ran and ran through the meadow, until they came to a cliff. Then she awoke with the strange sensation of having landed on the soft feather tick with a bump.

She lay a moment with her heart pounding. As she lay, reliving the nightmare, she heard the rustle of the door being opened and thought she was still dreaming. Her eyes flew open, and she stared into impenetrable blackness. She couldn't see a thing, but she felt, or imagined, a breeze, and she had a distinct awareness that she wasn't alone in the room. It wasn't a doubt, but a certainty. Someone was there, in the blackness just inside the door. She froze, not moving a muscle. There! Wasn't that a deep-drawn breath? She waited, but the sound was not repeated.

She was about to scream when she remembered Luten's letter in Susan's lap desk. He had come looking for it when he thought she was asleep! Into the shuddering silence came a light tread as the form advanced. She lay rigid, breath suspended, as he approached the bed. He walked right past it to the wardrobe. He was going to search the pockets of her gowns. She heard the door breathe open, followed by the susurration of gowns brushing against each other, the light scraping of hangers on the metal bar.

But what if it wasn't Luten? He wouldn't wait until she was in bed to search. He could come in any time when she wasn't there. Her heart pounded so hard she feared the intruder might hear it. She mentally gauged the distance to the door into the hall. Could she make it? Should she scream? The intruder didn't seem to be interested in molesting her. He might just take what he was looking for and leave without knowing she was there. He was looking for something.

She held her breath, waiting, ears strained for the softest sound in the shadows. As she became accustomed to the darkness, she could discern the outline of the man against the light wall. The shadow moved toward the dresser. A light jingle told her his hand had brushed Susan's trinket box. A drawer was quietly opened, then slid shut again. He turned and moved forward. As the intruder brushed past the bed, his hand moved out to touch it. When he felt her leg, he gave a frightened gasp. Not Luten, then. He knew she was in Susan's room. She opened her lips and screamed. He made a lunge at her. Fingers brushed against her face, then clamped over her lips. "Shhh!" he whispered in a frightened voice.

She wrenched her head aside and screamed as loud as she could. The man took to his heels, out the door and down the corridor. Any attempt at secrecy was abandoned. He pelted toward the front staircase and down the stairs. By the time she recovered and got out her door, Luten was just coming into the hall, carrying a lamp. He was still wearing his evening clothes. He hadn't retired yet, although it was the middle of the night.

"What happened?" he asked, hurrying forward.

"There was a man in my room!" she exclaimed.

Luten rushed toward her room. Corinne went after him. "He's gone now. He ran when I screamed."

He looked all around the room. "You were having a nightmare," he said.

"I was wide-awake! He was looking for something, Luten. Look, the wardrobe door is ajar. It was closed when I went to bed. He ran downstairs. Didn't you hear him running down the hall?"

"I only heard your bloodcurdling scream."

"There was someone here."

"I'll go down and have a look." He glanced around the room. "I see your window is closed. He didn't get in that way. I made sure all the doors were locked before I retired."

She snatched up a lacy negligee and threw it on. "I'm going with you. I want to see who it was." Before leaving, she picked up the poker. She knew Luten thought she was imagining things, but it was possible the intruder was still in the house.

She clung to Luten's arm as they went downstairs. He held the lamp high, looking all around the hall below. Long shadows moved lethargically as the lamp beam fell on the longcase clock, on chairs and a coatrack. When they were at the bottom of the staircase, they felt the draft from the front door and saw it was hanging open.

"I told you so!" she said.

Luten went and examined the door. "The lock doesn't seem to have been forced. How did he get in?"

"He must have a key. Who would have one?"

"He might have used a passe-partout. These old locks are not much protection." But he locked the door again, and they went into the saloon. Luten lit another lamp. He poured Corinne a glass of wine to calm her, and they sat on the sofa.

"I wonder what he was after," she said. "Was it just a coincidence that he went to Susan's room?"

When Luten saw her pale, distracted face, he knew that Corinne certainly believed she had had a visitor. He also knew that he wanted to comfort her with his warmth, to take her in his arms and kiss her fears away. He reached out his hand and squeezed her fingers.

"An ordinary thief would have gone for the silver," he said. "He wouldn't risk going upstairs. And if he did, he'd go to an empty room, one with the door open, not an occupied one. He knew where he was going, all right. If it was the kidnapper, who is to say he isn't after another victim? You're going back to London tomorrow morning, Countess."

That "Countess" got her back up. She snatched her

hand away. "Don't be an ass, Luten. He didn't know I was in Susan's room. And he wasn't looking for a kidnap victim in the clothespress. He seemed startled—frightened—when he felt me."

"Felt you?" he exclaimed. "What do you mean?"

"He just sort of touched the bed as he moved away from the dresser. I felt his hand on my leg, then he gasped. I screamed and he put his hand over my mouth to stop me."

"Did you get any inkling who he might be?"

"No, none. He was a biggish man."

"Could it have been Blackmore?"

She gave a sound of disgust. "It could have been anyone. He was looking for something, Luten. Is it possible Susan was mixed up in some dangerous business?"

"Like what?"

"Goodness, I don't know. First she disappeared—"

"She was kidnapped."

"We don't know that. She disappeared, then someone came sneaking into her room, looking for something. What I am wondering is if she discovered something, something dangerous. She had to be silenced, and now the man fears she left some evidence behind. It could be the highwayman," she said. "She might have found out who he is."

"We'll search her room."

"We've already searched it."

"We'll search it again tomorrow. We must have missed something. Drink up your wine. It's three-thirty. The sun will soon be rising."

She looked at his haggard face, and his evening jacket. "Why are you fully dressed? You haven't been to bed."

"I've been thinking."

"For four hours? You were out, Luten. Where were you?"

"I was spying on Blackmore. Looked in his windows like a Peeping Tom. He was up until two o'clock, reading and drinking brandy. Then he went up to bed. I saw the light go on in one of the bedrooms. I waited until it went off again and came back here."

"You're very troubled about Susan," she said, and watched him closely.

"If anything happens to her, I'll never forgive myself."

"She wasn't in your charge," she said.

"She was my cousin. Otto is no fit guardian. I feel responsible," was the only answer she got. She knew from long experience that there was no point trying to get information from Luten if he didn't want to give it.

"I see. You don't care to share your secret with me." Her emerald eyes glowed angrily. "Good night, Luten."

He rose and accompanied her upstairs. "It's not likely our intruder will come back tonight, but lock your door anyway, just in case," he said. "I'll leave mine open. I'll hear him if he returns."

He wouldn't be sleeping, in other words. What dark deed weighed on his conscience? Poor Luten. Poor Susan. Poor Corinne.

Chapter Fourteen

Despite her nightmares and her interrupted sleep, Corinne awoke early in the morning. She enjoyed having these few moments to herself. In London Mrs. Ballard would be rushing about, opening the curtains and asking what gown she wanted to wear and if she had enjoyed the party the night before. It had all seemed wildly extravagant at first, but now it had become a bore. Except for the morning cocoa or tea. A cup of tea would be nice now, before she dressed.

She opened the curtains to see what sort of a day awaited her. The sky was a brilliant azure arc, with not a cloud in sight. She threw open the window. Branches of oak and elm stirred in the warm breeze. A pair of larks performed aerial acrobatics, swooping and wheeling and soaring, with the sun glinting golden on their wings. A muslin gown would be warm enough. She'd wear her new rose sprigged muslin with the empire waist. She turned to the clothespress to take it out . . . and stared at the space where it had hung last night. She remembered she had put it beside the rose gown she had hung up.

The sprigged muslin was gone. The empty hanger jiggled mischievously in the breeze. She remembered the intruder last night, the quiet opening of that same door, the light chink of hangers on the metal bar. The man had stolen her gown! He had been an ordinary thief after all.

What else had he taken? She rushed about the room and found other items missing. Her new cashmere shawl—oh, and her reticule, with every penny she had brought with her. Silk stockings and underlinens were missing.

Her instinct was to run downstairs and tell Luten, but she had to dress first. There was no water in the water basin. She pulled the bell cord, but knew she would not be heeded. Too impatient to wait, she just threw on the same blue muslin gown she had worn the day before, scrabbled into shoes and stockings, ran a brush through her hair, and went darting to the morning parlor.

Luten, Prance, and a Coffen Pattle who looked as disheveled as she did herself arose punctiliously when she came pelting in. Luten and Prance looked as fine as ninepence. They had shaved, and their cravats were as immaculate and as intricately arranged as if they were on their way to Whitehall.

Prance took one look at her and said, "Not to give offense, dear heart, but don't you think you should send for Mrs. Ballard?"

"I've been robbed!" she announced.

"Luten has been telling us of your ghastly experience," Prance said, drawing out the chair beside him. "What a savage beast I am to have chastized you before commiserating on it. Small wonder if you look so . . . distraught."

"What's missing?" Luten asked her.

"He took my clothes."

Prance was charmed to hear it. "A pervert!" he exclaimed. "And I feared the country would be dull. As you are wearing that charming gown—again—one assumes it is your more intimate items that are missing. A petticoat thief!"

"No, my new rose-sprigged muslin gown and cashmere shawl. Oh, and my reticule with ten pounds in it, to say nothing of that darling little French hand mirror you gave me, Reg, and a few other small items."

"Gowns and gewgaws," Coffen said, frowning. "Strange sort of thief. He didn't touch the silver, and it wasn't even locked up as it should have been."

"I've been telling Prance and Coffen about your experience last night. We could find nothing missing down here," Luten said. "Tobin assures me the silver is intact."

As he spoke, his valet appeared at her elbow with a pot of coffee and a plate of breakfast. Simon had cooked breakfast and served it. This elegant creature held himself very high, but for a price, he had condescended to expand his duties. The coffee was black and hot. The poached eggs cooked *au point*, the toast neither black nor gray from ashes, but a nice golden brown. The bacon was crisp and not too fat. Even Prance, who felt eating was a great imposition on the intellectual life, was busy with his knife and fork, dismantling an egg.

"You're sure it was a man?" Prance asked her. "As everything taken was for a woman, one wonders if some local wench hasn't been ogling your gowns and decided to help herself to them."

"It was a man," she replied.

"Could have had her fellow steal them for her," Coffen suggested.

"One would think he could wait until the gown was hung out to dry," Prance said. "There was quite a rash of linen-napping from clotheslines in London last year. I lost half a dozen shirts. Strange that it should occur at this time, but it cannot have anything to do with Susan, can it? There is no limit to the reach of coincidence's long arm."

"I wonder if it has something to do with her," Corinne said, scooping her fork into her eggs. "She left the house

113

with only the clothes on her back. She must be wanting a change of gown by now. He wouldn't know, in the dark, that it was my gown he took. And how did he get in? The lock hadn't been tampered with."

"I could open that lock myself with a piece of wire," Prance said dismissively.

"What an accommodating kidnapper," Luten said, with a lift of his eyebrows. "As it was a man who stole the gown, presumably he did it for Susan."

"If that is the case, we need not fear that she is lying on a board in some cold shack, starving," Prance said.

"What you said last night, Prance," Coffen said. "About Soames having taken her and trying to talk her into marrying him."

"It was Corinne's theory that Soames took her. If she's right, I expect he is trying to talk her into marriage."

"Me, too. If that's what he's up to, he'd do whatever she said. Get her clothes for her if she asked him. I say we should have another go at Soames. There's something odd afoot. I had Eddie watch his place last night. He never went home. Where was he?"

Prance's eyebrows rose to his hairline. "You actually convinced Eddie to do your bidding?" he asked. "How much did you pay him?"

"A guinea. He only stayed until two A.M., but Soames hadn't come home. Where was he till that hour?"

"Perhaps helping himself to Corinne's gowns. It's worth a try," Prance agreed, and applied his knife and fork to a golden piece of toast. Eggs, he found, even well-cooked eggs, were too close to the barnyard to tempt him after all.

They were still at breakfast when Hodden arrived, hot from East Grinstead. He carried the staff of his office. Other than that, there was nothing to distinguish him

114

from a petty clerk or businessman. He was a smallish, well-knit man of some forty-odd years. His blue serge jacket had shiny cuffs, his buckskins were dusty, and his top boots lacked polish. His face bore some resemblance to a rabbit, due to his protruding teeth, but his snuff-brown eyes were as sharp as bodkins.

"News, milord!" he exclaimed, rushing into the morning parlor. When he had the undivided attention of the table, he continued. "He's struck again, the highwayman. A Mrs. Turner and her daughter from Dover were held up and relieved of a hundred pounds and their jewelry. A set of garnets and a pearl ring."

"What time?" Luten asked.

"Just after eleven. The villain cut their team loose. They had to walk three miles into town. By the time they got there, the scamp was long gone, of course."

"I might be able to give you a hand there," Coffen said. "I happen to know where he keeps his nag."

The snuff-brown eyes snapped angrily. "You might have told me, Mr. Coffen!"

"I'm telling you now, ain't I?"

"Well, where is it?"

"In the shepherd's hut."

"There are nine shepherd huts in the neighborhood. Which one?"

"At McArthur's burned-down place. I'll show you."

"I searched that little hut myself when we were looking for Miss Enderton. There was no mount there."

"Well there was last night. And I've a pretty good notion who your highwayman is as well. Do you have a nag or did you come on shank's mare?"

"I'm mounted," Hodden said proudly.

After some conversation, it was decided that all the gentlemen would accompany Hodden, in case Soames

115

put up a fight. Corinne didn't argue when Luten suggested rather imperatively that she stay at Appleby. She had a few investigations she wished to make closer to home.

Hodden's mount proved to be a mule, which slowed down their trip, but they did eventually reach the shepherd's hut. The mare was gone.

"We'll try young Soames's stable," Hodden said.

"You go ahead. I'll catch up with you," Coffen said. He went to look in the stream behind the hut. Trailing arms of willow dangled into the shade-dappled stream, where crystal-clear water gurgled over pebbles worn smooth by the water's passing. He walked a quarter of a mile in both directions from the hut, but found no corpse facedown in the water. He was vastly relieved, for he had had a nightmare the night before that Susan was drowned in this very stream.

He was about to leave when the flash of something red at the bottom of the stream caught his eye. He fished it out, wetting his sleeve to the elbow as the stream was deeper than it looked, and found it to be a brooch made of faux diamonds and rubies. Curious, he examined the stream more closely and found a few other bits of cheap imitation jewelry. A fish-paste pearl ring, a pinchbeck watch chain and fob, and a string of glass beads. Loot that the highwayman had discovered to be worthless after he had time to examine it closely. This confirmed that the missing mount belonged to the highwayman. It must be used only on those occasions when he planned a robbery, as there had been no mount there when Hodden searched. Perhaps the man rode through Grinstead on some other sort of mount and made his change here, which meant he had to sneak his scamp's nag into the hut earlier. Easy enough to do after dark, with the concealment of the trees along the stream. It definitely pointed to a local fellow.

All they had to do was put a watch on the spot and catch him when he came back. Coffen whistled for his mount, threw his leg over it, and rode after the others. They all agreed that the cheap jewelry proved the highwayman was using the shepherd's hut as a temporary hiding place for his mount.

When they reached Oakhurst, a modest mansion of stone, Mr. Soames's housekeeper seemed almost glad to see Hodden. She was a tall, genteel lady in a white cap, with a white apron over her black gown.

"How did you know?" she asked.

"Know what, Mrs. Peel?" Hodden replied in confusion.

"That he's missing. Mr. Soames didn't come home last night. I was just about to send the footman for you. He's not turned up dead!" she cried, and turned as pale as paper.

"He's not turned up at all, Mrs. Peel. We can't find him."

"He stopped at Appleby last night on his way home from the auction," Luten said. "He took dinner at the Rose and Thistle."

"He does that sometimes when he's late," Mrs. Peel said. "So considerate. What do you think could have happened to him?"

"It might be best if I have a look about the place," Hodden said. "It could give us an idea where he's gone. Could you show me his study, Mrs. Peel?"

She was all in a fluster at showing such a troupe about the master's house in his absence. She recognized the gentlemen, however, and knew that Luten was related to Soames. This seemed to set the seal on her approval.

"We won't trouble you further, Mrs. Peel. You can just go about your business," Hodden said in a kindly way.

"I'll make coffee," she said, and scurried off to the kitchen, happy for the diversion.

The gentlemen conversed quietly in Soames's modest study. "He's peeled off, it looks like," Hodden said. "I'll search his bedchamber. You, milord, might have a look over his account books and anything else that catches your interest. Letters, billets-doux, jewelry."

"I'll do the guest rooms," Prance said.

"I'll search his stable and barns," Coffen added.

After three quarters of an hour of searching, they met in the saloon, where Mrs. Peel had provided coffee.

"Thank you, Mrs. Peel," Hodden said. "I'll have a word with you before I leave."

She took the hint and returned to her kitchen.

"I found nothing suspicious," Hodden said. "There was no cache of money in his room, no hidden jewels."

"The timing of the robbery suggests Soames. He left the inn shortly before the Turner ladies were held up, but if he was the highwayman, you'd never guess it from his account books," Luten added. "He was skating close to the edge of bankruptcy. The mortgage his papa saddled him with was the culprit, I fancy."

"His own mount, the one he was riding last night, is in the stable," Coffen said. "The groom says it came home alone sometime during the night. Looks as if Soames might have taken a tumble and be lying in the road with a broken neck. Either that or he knows we're on to him and has shabbed off on the other mount."

Hodden looked in confusion from one to the other. "Mr. Soames had only the one mount in his stable," he said firmly.

"Perhaps he's not the highwayman," Prance said.

"I'm beginning to doubt he is, and I don't give a damn," Coffen said. "Did you find any sign he took Susan?"

"No, nothing," Luten and Prance said.

"What, kidnapped Miss Enderton!" Hodden exclaimed.

"Is that what you think? Oh, surely not. I could scarcely believe he was the highwayman but to do a thing like that! Soames was always a gentleman. He thinks the world of Miss Enderton. Why, for a while there, we expected a match between them."

"Are you sure he was at the fair that day she disappeared?" Coffen asked.

"He was. He left early, but it wasn't to kidnap Miss Enderton. He had an appointment with his banker."

"Did he keep it?" Coffen asked.

"I'll ask Fairly. That's our bank manager."

"Because if he didn't—if he's the one who took Susan, I mean—we might never find out where he's got her, now that he's disappeared. Sneaking her off to Gretna Green, I shouldn't wonder."

"He never took her," Hodden said angrily. "We must organize a group to scout about for Soames. The parish is becoming a regular den of vice, what with highwaymen and kidnappers and now this."

"We'll start searching now," Luten said.

"And keep an eye out for any sign of Susan while we're about it," Coffen added.

They discussed what direction each would take. It was, alas, Prance who found the mortal remains of Jeremy Soames, lying in a field half a mile from the road with his sightless eyes staring at the azure sky and his mouth fallen open in despair. The condition of his clothes and hands suggested that he had been trying to crawl home. The front of his jacket and his knees were well grimed, although he had turned over on his back to die. It was the bullet in his chest that prevented his making it home.

Prance had some instinctive notion that he shouldn't leave a corpse lying alone in a field, but common sense told him he must mount at once and fly to East Grinstead with this stunning news.

"Dead!" he would exclaim. No, "Murdered!" had a more dramatic ring to it. What a wretched soul he was, to be thinking of such a thing when poor Soames lay on the grass with his eyes and mouth open and his vest covered in congealing blood.

Chapter Fifteen

As soon as the gentlemen had left with Hodden, Corinne ran upstairs and begun to search the rooms. In the room next to Susan's bedchamber she found a cache of linen in the dresser. Half a dozen sets of new bed-sheets and pillowcases were there, not stitched by Susan's awkward fingers, but finely done by a seamstress. This confirmed the notion of a trousseau. In another spare room she found towels and an elegant lace tablecloth worth a small fortune. All these sat idle while the towels in the guest rooms were threadbare and the sheets on the beds were like tissue paper. One daren't turn over for fear of ripping them.

Excited, she next searched the attics, but she did not find the expected carpets or chaise longue, nor anything except old clothes and discarded lumber.

She planned to pay a morning call, but as her host was so exceedingly handsome, she wished to tidy her appearance. Simon proved vulnerable to flattery when she stopped at Luten's room to compliment him on the marvelous breakfast he had prepared them.

"I should have brought Mrs. Ballard with me," she said. "Here am I looking as if I had just run a smock race, while you turn Luten out in such high style. It is a problem even getting hot water. How do you manage it, Simon?"

"It will be my privilege to assist you, your ladyship," he said, wearing a smile from ear to ear.

Simon glided down to the kitchen and was back in minutes with a basin of hot water. He mentioned that he had a few leisure moments, and if her ladyship had anything she wished ironed, he would be only too happy to oblige her. And she was only too happy to hand her wrinkled gowns over to him.

Fifteen minutes later, a refreshed and more stylishly coiffed Lady deCoventry set out for Mr. Stockwell's house. Without Luten to hold her in check, she took the shortcut on foot down the path and across the park to Greenleigh and was soon tapping at his door.

"He rode out to his back acres an hour ago," Mrs. Dorman said. "He's fertilizing that field today, but I expect him back any moment, if you'd care to step into the parlor. A cup of tea, milady?"

"Thank you."

While Corinne sat waiting, there was a knock at the front door. As Mrs. Dorman was in the kitchen, Corinne answered it for her.

"Luten!" she exclaimed. A scowl settled on her face. She had hoped for a private interview with Stockwell. He would be less forthcoming with Luten there, glowering at him.

"What the devil are you doing, answering Stockwell's door?"

"Mrs. Dorman is making me some tea."

"Has Stockwell opened a tea parlor?"

"Not at all. He is tending to his work, like a good farmer." As they went into the parlor, she said, "You planned to come here without me! Don't deny it. You are supposed to be searching for Jeremy."

"The shoe is on the other food, Countess. You were supposed to be searching Appleby. Fortunately, Tobin saw you leaving. I decided you require a chaperon, as you obviously plan to seduce the poor innocent." His eyes skimmed over her, noticing her improved toilette. Her green eyes glowed like emeralds in the sunlight, but they didn't distract him from noticing she was pleased at that charge of dangling after Stockwell, and he was pleased that she enjoyed his jealousy.

"I would never seduce an innocent lad. I have some scruples. Now, if he cared to try his hand at seducing me, that is a different matter entirely."

He had to make a conscious effort to sound annoyed. "You are disgusting, Countess."

"What's sauce for the gander . . ."

"Must we wallow amongst clichés?" he asked in a bored drawl.

"Surely we require more than one for a good wallow?"

"Where is Stockwell?"

"Mrs. Dorman tells me he is fertilizing his back acres but should return presently."

"One does not usually greet a lady after fertilizing his fields with manure. Let us hope Stockwell takes time to refresh himself before he comes."

"I'm sure one may count on Mr. Stockwell to do all that is proper," she said.

A younger servant appeared with the tea tray. She was clean and bright-eyed. The tea tray, on this occasion, held the honey cake that had been missing on their last call.

"We are in a hurry," Luten said. "Could you direct me to this field where your master is working?"

"Oh, her ladyship wouldn't like that!" she said with a shy glance at Corinne. "I just saw his mount go into the barn as I left the kitchen. I'll go and hurry Mr. Stockwell along."

She set down the tea tray in front of Corinne, bobbed a curtsey, and left.

123

"You wanted me to see Mr. Stockwell in his working clothes," Corinne charged. "I daresay he looks magnificent with his broad shoulders stretching his shirt taut over his muscles."

"You forgot the perspiration beading his noble brow."

Corinne smiled as she handed him his tea. "I didn't forget it. Some thoughts are best kept to oneself." She drew a blissful sigh.

Luten polished his nails and glanced about the room.

Before he could think of a setdown, Rufus Stockwell was at the door. Corinne remembered him as an exceedingly handsome man, yet she was surprised anew at just how handsome he was. Not only handsome, but with the added charm of youth and vibrant health. He wore a blue jacket, buckskins, and top boots, untouched by fertilizer. He had obviously been overseeing his men at work, not personally shoveling manure. He bowed politely at them both, said "Good morning," then directed himself to Luten.

"Mrs. Dorman tells me you are in a hurry. Sorry to detain you. I have my men marling the back acres. The soil there is slightly acidic. I expect the carbonate of lime will improve the yield."

Corinne said, "Ah, you are one of the improving farmer breed, Mr. Stockwell. How clever of you."

"When one's acreage is small, he must optimize every inch," he said, and took a seat. "Is there any news of Miss Enderton?"

"I'm afraid not," Luten replied. "The reason I am here has nothing to do with Miss Enderton, not directly in any case. You heard that Soames was missing?"

"Missing? No, I hadn't heard it. I saw him yesterday."

"He didn't come home last night. Hodden had men out searching for him. His body was found in the meadow a mile from Oakhurst. He'd been shot."

Stockwell's eyes opened wide; his face paled, and he exclaimed, "Good God! Do they know who did it?"

"Not yet."

"The highwayman got him, I expect."

Corinne also exclaimed. "Soames murdered! You didn't tell me, Luten! Oh dear! What— Do you think it has anything to do with Susan's disappearance?"

"I have no idea, but if he was the one who has her hidden away, we'll have the devil of a time finding her now."

"Soames!" Stockwell said in consternation. "He'd never hurt Miss Enderton. He was fond of her. I really think you're looking up the wrong tree there, milord."

"The assumption in town is that he was the highwayman."

Stockwell laughed out loud. "Soames, turned highwayman?" he asked. "The highwayman's victim, more like. He had taken the notion of capturing the fellow, for the reward, you know. If he were the scamp, he wouldn't be so short of funds. He never paid me for the milcher— but this is no time to speak of that."

They discussed the murder a moment and the possibility of its being connected to Susan's disappearance. Stockwell was adamant that Soames had nothing to do with Miss Enderton's disappearance.

"I should hate to think of his good name being smeared in this manner when he isn't here to defend himself," he said.

Corinne fanned herself. She suddenly began weaving in her chair. Stockwell noticed it first.

"Lady deCoventry! I say—" He turned to Luten. "She seems faint. I'll get some brandy."

Corinne turned to Luten. "My hartshorn, Luten," she said in a weak voice. "I keep that bottle in the pocket of your carriage."

Luten flew out the door to fetch it. As soon as he was gone, she recovered from her imaginary fainting spell.

"Never mind the brandy, Mr. Stockwell. I had hoped for a word alone with you," she said. "I have some reason to believe Susan was in love with someone, perhaps even planning to marry. Would you have any notion who this man might be?"

"Marry?" he cried in alarm. But she noticed the idea of Susan's being in love came as no surprise to him. He looked more guilty than anything else. "No. No idea at all." He was a wretched liar. His cheeks were pink. "Why do you ask me?"

"I thought you might be the man she is in love with," she said, and gave him her most sympathetic smile. "I am sure no lady would be surprised if it were the case."

His face relaxed into a shy, boyish smile. "It is true I love her," he said, "but I know I could never marry her. She is worlds above me. I promise I have not importuned her in any way."

"But has she importuned you?"

"I . . . We have met a few times, by accident. She says she cares for me, but I . . . To tell the truth, milady, I am at my wits' end."

Before he could say more, Luten was back with the hartshorn, and Corinne was obliged to begin fanning herself faintly with her gloves, Luten noticed that her color was good. She had been talking in a low voice to Stockwell—and there was no sign of the brandy. What was the minx up to? She accepted the hartshorn and thanked him, uncapped it and applied it to her nose, but he noticed she didn't inhale.

"It was the shock of hearing that Jeremy is dead," she said to Luten. "Prance found him, you say? It must have been dreadful for him."

126

"Yes, for us all. If you are feeling better, Countess, we should go and let Mr. Stockwell return to his work."

Mr. Stockwell's face was rosy from his chat with Corinne as he accompanied them to the door.

"If there is anything I can do to help in finding Mr. Soames's killer, I hope you will let me know," he said.

When Luten and Corinne were in the carriage, he said, "Odd he is so eager to defend Soames and help find his murderer. I don't recall him offering to help find Susan, do you?"

"I'm sure he did. If he didn't, it was an oversight. It was taken for granted."

"He never mentioned looking for her, though. Everyone else one speaks to tells of searching his barns and the ditches."

"Mr. Stockwell is the strong, silent type."

"Then one can assume it was not his sparkling repartee that took you scampering across the meadow to visit. Why did you go to call on him?"

"To see if he had heard anything about Susan."

"And had he?"

"Of course not," she said testily. "But I think he was on closer terms with her than he has been letting on. In fact, I think the hussy has been hounding him to marry her." Luten gave a dismissing laugh. "You think it's only gentlemen who can make fools of themselves over a pretty face?" she asked.

"That is no way to speak of your late husband, Countess."

"I wasn't speaking of George, Luten."

"Why do you think Susan had been hounding Stockwell?"

"He spoke of what he called 'accidental meetings.' I sensed that she arranged these accidents."

127

"More likely he arranged 'em. But I doubt if he had anything to do with Soames's death."

"Are you now looking into that, as well as Susan's disappearance?"

"One can hardly ignore it. They are probably connected. Besides, he was my cousin. Finding Susan must have top priority, however. We have to find her before she's murdered, too."

Corinne uncapped the spirits of hartshorn and took a real whiff this time. Tears spurted to her eyes from the ammonia fumes. She thought over what Luten had said, that it was odd Stockwell never mentioned trying to find Susan. He had that moonish look of a man in love when he spoke of her. "I am at my wits' end," he had said. But instead of going out to search for her, he was at home, tending to his farm. She was sure Susan wanted to marry him.

"I wonder if he has the chaise longue sequestered at Greenleigh," she said. "It isn't at Appleby. It's perfectly clear he's madly in love with her."

"Am I to deduce you had no luck in seducing him?"

"I haven't tried." When she saw his grin, she added, "Yet. Next time I go, perhaps. I feel there is something fishy going on at Greenleigh, to say nothing of Appleby."

She told Luten about finding the linen and towels and lace tablecloth. "She was definitely assembling a trousseau. How sad if she never gets to use it. We must find her, Luten."

"You don't have to tell me."

He was wearing that anxious face again, suggesting he had Susan on his conscience. And now Soames's murder, to add another yarn to the tangled skein.

Chapter Sixteen

Susan's friends met up again at Appleby Court. As Mrs. Malboeuf's food was inedible, and as Simon could only be imposed on to a limited extent, the group decided to take lunch at the Rose and Thistle. Luten felt it would be good for Otto to get out of the house and urged him to join them.

"I'll stay home in case the ransom note comes," he said. "The bank delivered the ransom money this morning while you were out. I have been marking it."

Luten envisaged red X's on each bill. "Do you think that's a good idea, Otto?" he asked in alarm. "If the kidnapper notices the marks . . . How have you done it?"

"I didn't use a pen. I have been pushing a pin through the center of each bill and smoothing it out so he won't notice, but the little hole is there and can be found on a close examination."

"That's ingenious. You need a steady hand for that job. Don't take too much wine." It would take hours, but it gave Otto something useful to do and a reason to stay sober.

Otto pointed to the pot of tea on his desk. A bottle of wine sat beside it, but it was the tea he was drinking at the moment.

They left him to his job and went to the inn, where they

hired a private parlor to eat and discuss their morning's findings. Prance drew out his notepad.

"What do you think of this design for Blackmore's dinnerware?" he said, passing the pad along to Corinne. "It is only done in pencil, but envisage, if you can, a jet-black rim around the plate with a narrow gold band on the outer edge. Then the shield with a lion rampant. The crossed swords above refer to Blackmore's ancestors' probable place in the Celtic hierarchy. His coloring suggests that he is of Celtic origin. Their social system was divided into three parts, like Gaul. King, warrior-aristocrat, and freeman farmer. Blackmore's ancestors would have belonged to the second class, one assumes."

"Very nice," Corinne said. With her mind on more serious matters, her praise lacked enthusiasm.

"I expect you would prefer a dash of color. Blackmore, I feel, has more austere taste. There is nothing gaudy at Blackmore Hall." He immediately regretted that snide remark, but Corinne did not appear to connect it to her own love of ornamentation. It was Coffen who replied.

"Don't know why you waste your time doing free work for that scoundrel," he grouched. "It wouldn't surprise me if he was the highwayman and murdered poor Soames. I feel like the devil for having suspected Soames. We used to have good times together, coursing hares, riding, hunting. Let Blackmore design his own plates. Poor Soames will have no need of plates. I wonder if a fellow gets to eat in heaven."

"It will be no heaven for you if they don't," Prance said. "As to Blackmore, he is not a scoundrel! Luten was watching him at the time the Turner ladies were held up, so he cannot be the highwayman. We are assuming that is who murdered Soames. Did you think to ask Stockwell where he was last night when you were wooing him, Corinne?"

"No, I didn't know at the time that Soames had been murdered."

"You were with Stockwell when I told you," Luten reminded her.

"Yes, but I let off wooing him when you arrived."

"I would not say you had let off. You were gazing at him like a moonling."

Having excited a squabble, Prance said, "Now, now, children. No squabbling, *vi prego*."

"*Veepraygo?* What kind of talk is that?" Coffen scowled.

"It is Italian, Pattle. It is my admiration of Blackmore's Italian objets d'art that made it slip out." He turned to Luten. "Odd *you* did not ask Stockwell where he was last night, Luten, but then your mind was obviously on other things."

"Yes, I was considerably upset to learn of Soames's death," Luten said with an icy stare.

"That too." Prance smiled. "We'll let Hodden make the inquiries, shall we? He tells us no mysterious strangers have been seen in the neighborhood. I wonder if Soames's murderer could have been a woman. Perhaps he was playing some local belle false."

"His housekeeper says not," Coffen said. "He still had some hope of attaching Susan and was keeping his nose pretty clean in that respect. You keep your eyes open at Blackmore Hall when you take that picture over."

"What am I expected to find?"

"Clues. Letters. Anything belonging to Susan. You might take a peek into drawers and whatnot when he ain't looking. I don't suppose he opened his desk to you when he was giving you that tour?"

"Strangely, no," Prance said with great condescension. "We did not think it likely he had folded Susan up and

131

hidden her in a drawer. Nor do I intend to impose on his hospitality by sneaking behind his back to look today."

"He's too sharp to leave any clues about," Luten said.

They were just leaving the inn when Hodden came darting up to them, big with news. "A new development!" he exclaimed in some excitement. "I have found some evidence that Soames was our highwayman. I went back to his place and found these in a jewelry box in his late mama's room."

He held out a handful of trinkets—cheap glass brooches and rings.

"I saw them, but figured they were his mama's," Prance said. "What makes you think they're not?"

"They are on the list of items stolen by the highwayman. Hardly worth selling. He just tossed them aside and forgot them."

Coffen sighed and accepted that Soames was the highwayman. "No sign of a turnip watch?" he asked.

"None."

"He tossed a bit of trash like this into the stream—the things I gave you. I wonder why he kept these. Where do you figure he sold the good stuff?"

"Oh, London, very likely. He wouldn't risk placing it on the oak hereabouts. He used to go up to London every month on business or visiting relatives."

"Then it seems his murder had nothing to do with Susan," Corinne said.

"I figure he tried another robbery after he held up the Turners, his intended victim shot him and didn't report it," Hodden said. "To save himself trouble, he just rode off. If a man takes to robbing, he gets what is coming to him. P'raps this is better than the gibbet. I own I am surprised at Soames, but there you are. You never know what a decent-seeming fellow is up to behind your back."

"But what did he do with the money he stole?" Luten

asked. "Stockwell mentioned he still hadn't been paid for a milcher he sold Soames some time ago. He bought a used dung cart at Wetherby's sale. Hardly the act of a rich man."

"He could hardly start spending freely when the whole parish knew his pockets were to let. I expect the money is sitting safe in a bank in London drawing interest, waiting for some relative to die, so Soames could claim he had come into an inheritance. He was with Fairly, the bank manager, on fair day, making some arrangement about his mortgage. We cannot lay Miss Enderton's disappearance in his dish. Fairly was close as an oyster about Soames's business doing. Perhaps he was rearranging his mortgage."

"These baubles certainly are prima facie evidence at least that Soames was the highwayman," Prance said pensively.

"It don't do anything to help us find Susan," Coffen said. "As you've called on Stockwell, Corinne, I shall make a bunch of visits around town and see what I can ferret out. Vicar, modiste, milliner, that Miss Blanchard Susan used to visit. She might know something."

"I'll go with you," Corinne said. "What will you do, Luten?"

"Go back to Appleby and see if the ransom note has arrived. But first I'll send a note to Townsend of Bow Street to check up on the London banks for any account in Soames's name."

"Might he have used an alias?" Prance asked.

"How long has the highwayman been active in these parts?" Luten asked Hodden.

"Only six months."

"Townsend can make inquiries for any new accounts during the past six months. I'll send a description of Soames. And I'll have Townsend look into recent sales of jewelry as well. You said you have a list of items stolen, Hodden?"

"Indeed I do. At my office. You can write to Townsend from there. He'll take more notice of a lord. I've been in touch with Bow Street. Sent them a list of items stolen by the highwayman. A lady sold a few of the stolen pieces. Called herself Mrs. Bewley, from Northumberland. Townsend put a trace on her but could find no such lady. We figured she was the highwayman's doxy, or his wife or daughter. Did Mr. Soames have a lady friend in London?"

"No," Corinne said. "He usually asked us to introduce him to ladies. He used to stay with you, Luten." She looked a question at him.

Luten shook his head. "He'd hardly introduce us to a female of that sort."

Before leaving, Luten said to Corinne, "Try to get Simon to make dinner for us. You seem to have a way with him," he added with a knowing look. "I found him in the kitchen brushing your rose silk when I returned this morning to look for you."

"As you were complaining of my unkempt appearance, I didn't think you would mind."

"Not at all. It's my pleasure to hire servants for your use. Don't hesitate to ask him if he can do something with your coiffure."

"Too kind," she said through thin lips.

"Always happy to oblige, Countess." His smile told her it was all in jest. It was his rather strange way of courting her.

The group parted to go their separate ways. Corinne and Coffen had very little luck interviewing the locals. Miss Blanchard, a pretty provincial lass, did corroborate what Corinne suspected, that Susan had a tendre for Stockwell.

"She was ever so fond of him, but she got nowhere. Stockwell was too proud."

Coffen took umbrage on Susan's behalf. "Susan is plenty good enough for him! Too good."

"That's what he said, that she was too high for him, being related to fine lords and ladies. Rufus is very proud, in his own shy way. He didn't want anyone saying he was overreaching himself. But he liked her ever so much. He couldn't keep his eyes off her. He'd never harm a hair of her head. He treasured that bookmark she made for his birthday as if it were gold."

"Bookmark, you say?" Coffen asked, eyes narrowed. Then he turned to Corinne. "I thought you said she made him slippers."

"No, she bought him blue slippers at the Christmas bazaar, but I believe she told him she made them herself. Susan's a poor knitter. You're out if you think he had anything to do with her disappearance," Miss Blanchard said.

"We don't suspect him of having any evil intentions," Corinne assured her.

"Did she ever make hankies?" Coffen asked.

"Yes, but she thought they weren't good enough for Rufus and sent them to someone else."

Coffen sighed and bid farewell to his dream of marrying Susan. He and Corinne soon left.

Prance had a more fruitful visit. Blackmore did not appear to be expecting him. In fact, the butler was loath to admit Prance. But Prance had a way with servants. If he disliked what they were saying, he ignored them. He handed the butler his curled beaver, his malacca walking stick and York tan gloves, and sauntered into the saloon unannounced.

If Blackmore was not eager to see him, he hid his

vexation like a gentleman. He greeted Prance politely enough and offered him a glass of excellent sherry.

"I have been working on the design for your dinnerware," Prance said, handing over the pad and hovering nearby to accept praise. "This is a very rough sketch, of course. I would work it up in color, but alas! I did not bring my watercolors with me. Really it should be done in oils to bring out the richness of the colors. Watercolors would not do them justice. There is no getting a jet-black from watercolors. As to the gold—"

Blackmore expressed appreciation, and they sat down to talk.

"You have heard the news?" Prance asked.

"About Soames's murder? Yes, I heard it. The highwayman got him, I expect."

"*Al contrario!* You have not heard the cream of it. Soames *was* the highwayman."

Blackmore was perfectly silent. He sat blinking in astonishment for a moment, then said, "Are you sure?"

"You are shocked, as we all were, but there is some pretty damning evidence. Hodden found some of the stolen trinkets in his house. Tawdry things that were not worth selling. He was a fool not to have got rid of them, but there. I never did think Soames particularly bright. Truth to tell, I would not have credited him with the nous to run this rig."

"Nor did I."

Prance noticed that Blackmore was ill at ease; his eyes kept shifting about, often glancing off the surface of the sofa table. Prance wondered what caused his *gêne*. He followed Blackmore's darting gaze and noticed there was another wineglass on the table. It had been used. Soon he noticed something even more telling—a pair of dainty blue kid gloves, only partially concealed by a magazine. The rogue in him was delighted to have caught Blackmore

136

out in an indiscretion. She must be a married lady, or why the secrecy?

He gave Blackmore a knowing smile. "We are not children, my dear Blackmore," he said archly. "You may introduce your *chère amie* to me. I am not one to cast a stone, or more importantly, to spread gossip."

Blackmore tossed back his head and laughed. "In that case, my—niece, shall we say?—will be charmed to meet you."

The thing went from good to better. The lady was right in the room, hiding behind the curtain. And when she came out, laughing in embarrassment, she was seen to be utterly delightful, as any *chère amie* of Blackmore's was bound to be. Beneath a tousle of black curls, a pair of blue eyes gleamed with the coquettish charm of the born flirt. This would be the beauty the youngsters had seen when peeking through Blackmore's windows. Her blue gown of watered silk had no hint of the provinces. Its rather daring neckline suggested a French modiste. At close range, she was seen to be a little older than the coiffure and youthful gown suggested. Prance felt no lady over five and twenty ought to wear pastel hues, but she was by no means hagged. The overall impression was of a ripe peach, ready for plucking.

"Mrs. Spencer, may I present Sir Reginald Prance," Blackmore said.

Prance rose and lifted her white fingers to his lips. "Charmed, madam. It lacked only this to make a delightful visit memorable. Had I the good fortune to be your patron, I would not hide you behind a curtain, I promise you." He directed a leering, playful smile at Blackmore. He showed the lady to a chair, lifted his coat-tails, and resumed his seat.

"We weren't sure who our caller was," Blackmore explained. "The vicar has been pestering me to donate a stained-glass window to the memory of my parents. I really ought to do it." He continued to Mrs. Spencer, "Sir Reginald is visiting at Appleby Court. He is a friend of Susan's."

"Such a shocking thing!" she exclaimed. "The poor girl."

"Do you know Miss Enderton?" Prance asked, in a subtle attempt to discover what he could of Mrs. Spencer.

"I have met her occasionally in Town. I'm not from the neighborhood, Sir Reginald. Just rusticating in the countryside for a spell."

"Ah." The syllable was fraught with curiosity, but she chose not to enlighten him by much.

"I am originally from London," she said. "I dropped in this afternoon to have a word with my cousin, Blackmore."

Blackmore chewed back a grin. "That's uncle, Mrs. Spencer," he said, and they all uttered a sophisticated laugh.

"I shall soon be returning to London myself," Prance said, with another hopeful smile.

"Alas, it is not likely we shall meet," she replied vaguely. "I go about very little nowadays."

"It is Society's loss," Prance said, bowing his head.

His glass was empty. Blackmore did not offer to refill it. When neither the host nor Mrs. Spencer said anything, Prance took the hint and arose.

"I must not interrupt your little tête-a-tête," he said. "If I had realized . . . *Scusatemi*. Strange, I find myself speaking Italian when I am in your house, Blackmore. It is the air of culture."

"Always delighted to see you, Sir Reginald," Blackmore said, rising to accompany him to the door.

When they were in the hallway, Prance said with a waggish look, "Blackmore, you sly dog. She is charming.

Simply exquisite. Why do you not rush her to the altar at once?"

"Because she is married already. Unhappily, of course. I hope I am not one to break up a happy marriage. Her husband is an MP. Denise is . . . ah . . . visiting her aunt during Mr. Spencer's sojourn in London. I know I may count on your discretion."

"Mum's the word—uncle. Or do I mean auntie?"

Pleased with his little joke, he left.

As he drove home, thinking of Mrs. Spencer, he began to believe he had seen her somewhere before. Probably at some dull MP's do. A charmer. Trust Blackmore. Where had he met her? She wasn't a local lady, or she would be better acquainted with Susan. They had both been very secretive about it. Perhaps the husband was a Tartar. It pretty well exonerated Blackmore of any interest in Susan. Who would bother with the chit when he had such an Incomparable under his protection?

As his visit had been cut short, he decided to return to East Grinstead and met up with Corinne and Coffen. He kept his word and mentioned nothing of Mrs. Spencer. It took a sharp effort, for he loved gossip nearly as much as he loved new jackets, but he said only that Blackmore had loved the design for the dinnerware.

"He was busy, so I didn't stay," he said.

No one asked what he had been busy at, so no lies were necessary. They returned to Appleby Court together.

Chapter Seventeen

When Luten returned from East Grinstead, he brought with him the broadsheets announcing Susan's disappearance and offering a reward of ten thousand pounds.

"Ten thousand pounds!" Prance exclaimed. "We agreed on half that sum, Luten. You offered two thousand, and the rest of us—Corinne, Coffen, and myself—one thousand each. Much as I love dear Susan, I am not sure I can afford—"

"I expect Otto kicked in the other half, from Susan's own money, I mean," Corinne said, looking to Luten.

"I donated the other five myself," Luten said, with a perfectly wooden face.

"Will Susan repay us if we get her back?" Prance asked.

"I am hardly in a position to ask her," Luten said curtly. "If you don't wish to contribute, Prance, no one is forcing you. I'll make up the difference myself."

"No, no. Count me in. I was just asking."

"Otto will pay the ransom, if a ransom note comes," Luten explained. "These broadsheets have to be distributed. Hodden is seeing to it in East Grinstead. We should fan out around the neighborhood. Hodden says we have only to deliver them to the constable in each town, and he will see that they're posted. I plan to head to the coast. I'll cover the towns and villages between Hastings and

Brighton, spending the night at my Brighton house. Coffen, you cover the northwest, Prance the northeast."

"What about me?" Corinne asked.

"Look after Otto," Luten said. "And keep your eyes and ears open here. Hound Hodden. Question anyone you can think of."

"Since it seems we must stay overnight in some ghastly village inn, I shall take my valet," Prance said. "I wish I had brought my own bedsheets with me."

"I'll pack a few things," Coffen said, and ambled off to do it.

The gentlemen all left to make their preparations. Corinne picked up the broadsheet Luten had brought in to show them. The rest were in his carriage. Each of the gentlemen would take a stack of them with him. She read the fateful words. The top lines were done in heavy black print to attract attention.

MISSING: TEN THOUSAND POUNDS REWARD FOR INFORMATION LEADING TO RECOVERY. The description of Susan followed. Susan Enderton, of Appleby Hall, East Grinstead. Female, twenty years of age, blond hair, blue eyes, five feet four inches, weight one hundred and ten pounds approximately. Missing from her home on May 5. It went on to mention that she had been wearing a blue gown.

Seeing it in black and white made it all worse, somehow. Inevitable, like an epitaph. It rendered Susan anonymous; the description might refer to any young blond lady. It diminished her to a few words on paper, like a stranger. One saw these bills all over England, glanced at them, shook her head, and forgot them. One never realized the anguish they represented to the family and friends, to say nothing of the victim.

Where could she be? A girl didn't just disappear off the face of the earth. If she had been kidnapped, there would have been a ransom note, so she must have been carried off by some mad sex fiend. Yet there had been no strangers seen around Appleby. It had been fair day, but why would a man come out to a private estate to steal a girl when the town would have been full of attractive farm girls and servants? A stranger wouldn't know Susan was in the habit of sitting in the orchard. It wasn't even visible from the road, and there was no public path that would have given him a chance view of Susan.

It didn't seem logical. It must have been someone from the neighborhood who knew her and had secretly lusted after her. Blackmore, Soames, Stockwell. Soames was dead. Blackmore and Stockwell had been at the fair. Why had her sewing basket been chucked into the tree? Had she put it there herself? Had her kidnapper? If so, why? It didn't make sense. None of it made any sense. Even if she had been enceinte and run away of her own accord, it still didn't make sense.

If she didn't love the father, if she had been violated, she would have reported the man. And if she loved him, she would have gone after him and made him marry her. Susan was no longer a biddable child. She had a new way of "putting her little foot down." What if she had fallen in love with a married man? But there was no married man in the neighborhood so attractive that a girl would throw all her scruples to the wind and give herself to him.

The only man that attractive was Rufus Stockwell. She was interested in him, and he loved her madly. If he had ruined her, he would certainly have done the right thing by her.

Lastly, Corinne thought of Luten. Of his anguished face when he had heard of her disappearance and the haunted look he had worn ever since. It was weighing on his conscience, he said. He and Susan had been exchanging letters, letters about which he was extremely secretive. He had offered seven thousand of his own money to find her. He was wealthy, but seven thousand pounds was still a fortune. And he had tried to hide the trousseau in the chest in her room. When was the last time Luten had seen Susan? It must be half a year ago. If she was pregnant by him, her condition must have been obvious, but no one had mentioned it.

Was it even remotely possible that Luten had had his way with her? Was that what the letters were about? "Pray don't be angry with me, Luten," she had written. Angry because she was carrying his child? That she was pushing him to marry her? Or even that she was refusing to marry him, because she loved Rufus? And did any of it have anything to do with Soames?

When she heard a sound in the hallway, she looked up and saw Luten gazing at her. He held a small valise in his hand, ready to leave. He stepped into the saloon, still wearing his pale, haunted look.

"When was the last time you saw Susan, Luten?" she asked.

"At the end of February," he replied. "Why do you ask?"

If she were only two and a half months pregnant, it wouldn't be visible yet. "Just curious. I haven't seen her since last May, when she visited me in London. Just for a few days. Where did you see her in February?"

"Here, at Appleby."

"You never mentioned it! Why did you come here?"

"I believe I mentioned attending Clarence Moore's wedding in Horsham. While I was so close, I stopped in to visit Susan and Otto. I stayed overnight. The weather was wretched. I didn't like to head out to London at eventide."

"I see. How did she seem then?"

He shrugged. "Just as usual. Perhaps a little peevish.

143

She had wanted to visit Miss Blanchard in town that day, and the weather kept her home."

A stormy night, the two of them virtually alone in the house, for Otto would have been in his cups by evening. Susan in a peevish mood, Luten trying to cheer her up. Yes, it could have happened. Luten's cool veneer hid a passionate nature, as she had occasion to know.

Her voice, when she spoke, betrayed none of her racing thoughts. "You were generous to offer such a large reward."

He batted his hand, as if seven thousand pounds was a mere bagatelle. "I may inherit her fortune, God forbid."

"Really? I didn't know that."

"Nor did I, until this trip," he said, advancing into the room. "Coffen told me after Soames's death. You recall they left their estates to each other, so if Susan is dead, if she died first, Soames's heirs will end up with the lot. If Soames died first, Coffen will inherit Appleby, with a proviso that Otto can live here until his death, with a small income from the estate. And you will get her jewelry. In any case, it will be a heyday for the solicitors."

"I had no idea what was in her will. We were her nearest and dearest, then." Especially Luten. He was to get thirty-five thousand. At least she had no fear that Luten had done Susan in. Not only had he been in London when she disappeared, but he had no need of her money.

"Try not to worry, Corinne," he said, moving closer and reaching for her hands. "We'll find her." But it was Luten who was more worried. His eyes were dark, and his face was drawn from prolonged anxiety. Her heart went out to him.

"God, I wish this were over, one way or the other," he said in a choked voice, and drew her into his arms. When she gazed up at him, she sensed a softening mood creeping

144

over him. He studied her with his dark gray eyes, then said, "If it weren't for you, I don't think I could have stood it." When he pressed her close against him, her world suddenly returned to sanity. He didn't love Susan after all. Surely he didn't. It was guilt that rode him.

"We're all terribly distressed, Luten, but you seem . . . shattered," she said, peering up at him.

"Small wonder if I am. It's my fault."

She tried to tame the rampant curiosity that raged forth at his words. "Why? Why do you say that?"

"It's a long story. . . ."

The sound of Prance and Coffen descending the staircase caused them to draw apart.

"No, you take the west as agreed, Pattle," Prance was saying in a querulous voice. "I have friends at Tunbridge Wells where I can stay the night. You know how I loathe public inns. I shan't sleep a wink. You always sleep like a log." Coffen grumbled his agreement. "Are we all set to leave?" Prance asked, as he entered. His sharp eyes examined Corinne and Luten closely. "Are we interrupting the leave-taking?" he asked archly. "Don't mind us, children. Kiss her good-bye, Luten, and let us be on our way. Parting is such sweet sorrow."

"We should be back tomorrow afternoon, Corinne," Luten said, but his eyes said more. "Take care. I'll just say good-bye to Otto before I go. Try not to let him drink too much."

"What if the ransom note comes while you're gone?"

"Whatever you do, don't deliver the money yourself. Send for Hodden. And sleep in some other bedroom tonight, in case our intruder returns. I've given orders that the grooms are to be on the *qui vive*."

"*Adieu, cara mia,*" Prance said, and gave her a loud smack on the cheek.

"We're off. Take care," Coffen said.

Corinne was alone, staring at the hated broadsheet. The house seemed like a mausoleum. The sun was shining, luring her outdoors. She took up a shawl and went out into the park to think. She wanted to go to the apple orchard, to the secret spot where she and Susan used to go, but that was where the man had got Susan. It was too isolated. Corinne strolled down through the park toward Greenleigh. Everything was so peaceful here, with the greenery all around and the tall trees swaying overhead. It seemed the last place in the world for such wicked goings-on as kidnapping and murder.

Stockwell was just dismounting from his gig. She waved to him and hurried forward. He waved back, then gathered up some parcels from the back of the rig and walked to meet her. As she moved toward him, she was struck again by how handsome he looked with the sun on his golden hair. He had left his curled beaver in the rig.

"Any news of who might have shot Soames?" he asked.

She shook her head, then told him about the stolen items found in his house.

"It seems he was the highwayman after all," she said.

A frown grew between his brilliant blue eyes. "That's hard to believe. Soames was bound and bent to find the highwayman and collect the reward. He was forever snooping about the countryside. I wonder if he didn't find the trinkets in the shepherd's hut where they'd been left by the highwayman."

"Would he not have turned them over to Hodden?"

"I expect he wanted to capture the villain himself, to make sure he got the reward. Mrs. Dorman told me about Mr. Coffen's leading Hodden to the hut. No doubt I would have heard about Soames being suspected, if the ladies at the drapery shop had not all been gossiping about Mrs. Spencer."

Corinne had no interest in inconsequential village

gossip. "I believe you're right, Mr. Stockwell!" she exclaimed. "Or perhaps Soames found the gewgaws in the stream. Coffen found some similar trinkets there. I should tell Hodden!"

"I'll go back to Grinstead myself. I can convince him, as Soames spoke to me about it a dozen times."

"Hodden won't be happy to hear it. He's very pleased to think he's solved the mystery of the highwayman."

She went on to tell him that the others had gone to distribute the broadsheets. He listened, frowning deeply. It struck her as odd that Stockwell hadn't inquired about Susan. After all, he was supposed to be mad for her.

"It's odd there's been no ransom demand, don't you think?" she said.

"I daresay it is. Yes, that looks suspicious."

"It seems very strange to me. It means she was either kidnapped for some other vile purpose than money or ran off on her own.

Stockwell's handsome face clenched into a frown. "Poor Mr. Marchbank. What a wretched thing for him to be put through. It's unconscionable. Something must be done about it."

Not poor Susan, but poor Otto! "Her relatives and friends are doing everything they can."

"Oh, certainly! I did not mean to disparage Lord Luten—all of you in the Berkeley Brigade."

Now, how did Rufus, living deep in the country, know that Society called them that? It had obviously come from Susan.

The parcels he was holding began to sag in his arms. One fell to the ground. As he was so laden, Susan picked it up for him. It was a bag of sugarplums.

Stockwell saw where she was looking and said with a

147

shy smile, "It is Sally's—my maid's—birthday. The sugar-plums are a little present for her."

"That's thoughtful of you, Mr. Stockwell."

"It was Mrs. Dorman's idea. Well, I must be going. Good day, Lady deCoventry. I shall deliver my parcels to Mrs. Dorman before I go into town to speak to Hodden." He shook his head in disbelief. "Soames a highwayman! Did you ever hear such foolishness? Next they will take into their heads that I am the robber." There was an air of escape to his departure.

There was something she had never considered. Was it possible the handsome, shy Rufus had turned scamp to accumulate money to marry Susan? No, he would not have been so insistent on Soames's innocence if he were guilty himself. He would be happy to let the matter rest. Unless, of course, he planned to continue his marauding ways. . . . Oh, it was all too confusing! She returned to the house and made up a bed in one of the spare rooms. She didn't want a repeat of last night's intrusion. Sleeping would be hard enough with so much on her mind.

Chapter Eighteen

No ransom demand arrived at Appleby Court that evening. Otto drank too much, despite Corinne's efforts to dissuade him. She asked him about Luten's last visit at the end of February, but Otto's recollections were hazy.

"Susan was happy to see him," he said. As he could add no details, she assumed this was conjecture rather than memory.

She spent a weary evening worrying and thumbing through the journals without really reading them, and retired at eleven.

As if to mock her gloomy mood, the weather continued sunny the next morning. To avoid getting the megrims from sitting around moping, she took Susan's mount out, accompanied by a groom so that she could ride through spinneys and such isolated spots, looking for a trace of Susan. She found nothing, but the ride did improve her spirits. A hundred shades of green dazzled the eye: the luminous tips of tall trees, bathed in sunlight, the dappled grass beneath her feet, the deeper pockets of green in the glens, lightening to golden green in the distant shadows. She might have been back in Ireland.

In the afternoon she drove into East Grinstead, ostensibly to buy a pair of stockings to replace those stolen by the intruder. She had borrowed the money from Prance. Her real reason for going to Grinstead was to look at the broadsheets proclaiming Susan's abduction. The notices were garnering a good deal of attention. Small groups stood about, talking and gesticulating, even laughing. Well, it wasn't their tragedy. Life went on. If anyone in town knew anything about Susan's disappearance, he would not be slow to come forward now, with the lure of ten thousand pounds to tempt him. But when Corinne called on Hodden, he told her sadly that no one had come forward.

"Mr. Stockwell called on you yesterday afternoon?" she asked.

His snuff-brown eyes, like his voice, held an air of belligerence. "He did. I cannot think there is anything in his tale. Why would Soames not have turned the evidence over to me if he were innocent? No, Soames is our highwayman, milady." He drew a sheet of paper from the pile on his desk to suggest that he was a man of many affairs, too busy to sit chatting. "Remind Sir Reginald and Coffen they will be required to give evidence at the inquest this afternoon," he said in a dismissive way.

"They're out of town."

"I know it well. They will be back by four. They spoke to me before leaving. The inquest is delayed on their account. Their evidence is crucial."

"I shall remind them."

Next Corinne went to the drapery shop to buy the silk stockings. She met Mrs. Dorman there, sorting through the ribbons.

"I am looking for a birthday gift for Sally," she said, after greeting Corinne. "Her birthday is coming up next week."

"Next week? I thought it was yesterday."

"Now, wherever did you get that notion?"

"Mr. Stockwell mentioned he was buying her sugar-plums."

150

"Sugarplums for Sally? She'll not thank him. She is trying to lose weight. She's a little plump. No, I dropped him the hint she would like a tea set. She has a beau on the string and is gathering her wedding chest. He asked me to pick it out for him. The men are no good at that sort of thing, you must know."

"But he bought sugarplums yesterday."

"They would be for himself, but he was ashamed to admit it," she said, laughing. "Mr. Stockwell has developed a great sweet tooth lately. Odd, for he never much cared for sweets before. It is worrying about Miss Enderton that causes it, I expect. I always find a sweet helps ease sorrow, don't you?"

"Yes, I daresay you are right." Mrs. Dorman's eyes slewed over Corinne's shoulder to an elegant lady who was examining the muslins. Mrs. Dorman's expression held a glint of curiosity. "There is Mrs. Spencer, out shopping again," she said.

Corinne looked and saw a very dasher of a lady with black curls, outfitted in a handsome blue walking suit. "I don't recall seeing her before. Is she new in the parish?"

"She landed in on us last winter. She has hired that little cottage at the end of the High Street. A friend of Lord Blackmore, I believe." She gave a knowing nod to indicate what sort of friend. "She claims to have a husband in London, but we have seen no sign of him. You wouldn't want to have anything to do with the likes of her, milady. She could be wearing a tiara and the word *light-skirt* would still be written all over her."

They chatted awhile, then Corinne bought her silk stockings and took her leave. Out on the street, she met Coffen and Pattle, just back from their trip and looking fatigued. Their shirt points were wilted, and their jackets creased.

151

They had stopped to read one of the broadsheets. They rushed up to her and asked in unison, "Any news?"

"No, none," she said. "You have heard nothing either?"

"The constable at Tunbridge Wells thought he was on to something," Prance said. "A blond lady was found drowned in a pond outside of town, but she turned out to be a local light-skirt. I viewed the mortal remains." He shivered delicately. "The stuff of nightmares. She looked quite like Susan, too, or perhaps it is only that death robs us of our individuality."

"I wish you will stop your chatter," Coffen said gruffly. "You're giving me goose bumps."

"There is a new development in the highwayman case," Corinne said, and told them Stockwell's idea that Soames had found the trinkets in the hut or the stream behind it. "Hodden refused to consider it."

"You're on to something there," Coffen said at once. "I never could believe Soames . . . mean to say, a gentleman, even if he was poor as a church louse."

"That's mouse, Coffen," Prance said, shaking his head. "Must you always make fritters of the King's English?"

"Would a church louse be any richer?" Coffen asked, unfazed.

As they were talking, Mrs. Spencer came out of the drapery shop. Prance spotted her and quickly reviewed what etiquette demanded in this instance. Obviously he could not present a light-skirt to Corinne. He decided to lift his hat and smile, as he might do for any pretty lady passing by. It was a small town after all. Acknowledging her presence did not necessarily show that he had made her acquaintance. He lifted his hat; she gave him a bold smile and passed without speaking.

"That is Mrs. Spencer, a new dasher in town," Corinne said, as Coffen was staring after her.

"That ain't her name," Coffen said at once.

Prance looked at him, his eyes bright with curiosity. "Do you have the lady's acquaintance, Pattle?"

"I can't say I do, but she's no lady. That's Prissy Trueheart."

"Who?"

"Prissy Truehart. She used to be at Covent Garden a decade ago."

"She married a Mr. Spencer, MP," Prance said.

"I take leave to doubt it," Coffen said. "She is nothing else but a—" He glanced at Corinne.

"An actress?" she ventured, as Coffen was familiar with all the actresses. He was an avid habitué of the Green Rooms in London.

"That as well," he said.

"Oh! You mean a light-skirt."

"Are you sure?" Prance asked, looking after the dasher.

Coffen looked, too. "Ladies don't swing their rumps like that," he said condemningly, but he watched her out of sight.

Prance kept looking as well, not without admiration. Wife of an MP indeed! If such a delicious scandal had occurred within the past decade, he would have heard of it. Was it possible Lord Blackmore had been conning him? Or had the dasher been deceiving Blackmore? He was thrilled with the operatic vulgarity of it all. Should he mention it to the baron? And was he now free to tell the others? No, he would speak to Blackmore first. He had given the man his word.

"She arrived in East Grinstead last winter," Corinne said. "She lives in that little house at the end of High Street. The *on dit* is that she is Blackmore's mistress."

Prance was sorry he had held his tongue. Now that the secret was out, he could display his knowledge by saying, "Yes, I met her yesterday *chez* Blackmore. Charming girl."

"Hardly call her a girl," Coffen said. "She was on the boards aeons ago. Old Lord Clyde had her under his protection. The word was that she forged a check for a thousand pounds in his name, so he dumped her. She didn't get any takers after that. So this is where she washed up. She's still a looker."

"I should warn Blackmore," Prance murmured.

"I fancy Blackmore can look after himself," Coffen said.

"I wonder if I shouldn't replace that lion on his dinnerware with a satyr. I'll do it, just for a joke." He giggled to himself at his daring.

Coffen was frowning into his collar. "She hit town about six months ago and she lives in that little house on the edge of town, did you say, Corinne?"

"Yes, that is what Mrs. Dorman said."

"That's not far from the shepherd's hut. She might have seen the highwayman going into it. It was about that time that he started his nasty work."

Prance said, "Hodden has spoken to all the neighbors. If she knows anything, he would have got it out of her."

"Might not have," Coffen said. "The woman is crooked as a dog's hind leg. It wouldn't surprise me if she is in league with the highwayman, for a price. I'll have a word with Hodden before the inquest. It is at four o'clock. Are you going to attend it, Corinne?"

Prance said, "Lord, how I abhor such morbid doings. I shall make a quick dart to Appleby, bathe, and change my linen."

"You haven't time," Coffen told him.

"I shall take time. If I make a grand entrance late, I

154

shall at least look my best. I don't advise you to go, dear heart," he added to Corinne. She hesitated a moment. "I daresay Luten will be back by now," he added.

That was enough to secure her company. She sent Susan's carriage home without her and drove with Prance, while Coffen went to bend Hodden's ear.

"I am vexed with Blackmore for misleading me about Prissy Trueheart," he said. "Now, what the deuce is a chit like that doing in East Grinstead? She is not only an actress, but a known felon. You don't think she could be involved in Susan's abduction?"

"Surely not. There was no ransom note."

"We always come back to that, do we not? No ransom note. Well, we can hardly suggest to Hodden that Prissy abducted Susan for lustful reasons. He wouldn't know what we were talking about. I don't believe it myself, come to that. She bats her eyelashes too shamelessly at gentlemen. But she might still be involved in the highwayman business. It would be good to clear Jeremy's name."

"Yes, Hodden did not believe what Stockwell told him."

"It makes Hodden's life easier if he can pretend he has taken care of the highwayman. He'll claim the reward. I have half a mind to hold up a coach myself, just to prove it was not Jeremy. I expect it would only throw the parish into a pelter. Someone would swear an affidavit it was Jeremy's ghost, and a legend would be born. I shall mention it to Luten all the same."

"What we should do is force Hodden to search Mrs. Spencer's house."

"For clues, as Pattle would say. Perhaps it would be better not to alert her and put her on her guard, but just keep an eye on her ourselves."

When they arrived at Appleby Court, they forgot about Mrs. Spencer. At last, the ransom note had arrived.

155

Chapter Nineteen

Corinne could feel the difference in the very air of the house when she entered. Things had changed; there was a quickening, a sense of hope, that had not been there before. Or was it that she knew Luten was back? She saw his curled beaver on the hat rack even before he came from the saloon to greet her. It gave her time to compose her eager smile to mere pleasure. Old habits die hard.

"Luten, you're back."

He bowed. "Corinne. Prance." At closer range, she saw the excitement glowing in his eyes. For a brief moment she thought it was pleasure at seeing her, and her heart leapt. Then he spoke again. "The ransom note has come."

"Oh, let us see it!"

"Our trips were for naught," Prance said on a weary sigh. But of course, he was interested in the note and demanded to see it at once.

They went into the saloon. Luten placed the note on the sofa table so that they might all study it. It was printed on a sheet of plain white notepaper, not the very cheapest of paper, but not particularly fine either. It said:

Mr. Marchbank:

    Miss Enderton is alive and well. If you want her back, bring twenty-five thousand pounds in bills to the split oak at the northern edge of the Ashdown Forest tonight at midnight. Come alone. If you do exactly as I say, she will be home unharmed by one o'clock.

They all read it and fell silent. It was Prance who broke the silence. "Anyone might have sent this. There is no proof he has Susan."

Luten placed a little pearl ring on the table. "This came with it. It's Susan's."

Corinne picked up the ring, a little flower of gold with a pearl in the center. She had seen it dozens of times. "Yes, this is Susan's," she said. "Thank God she is unharmed."

"If we can believe that note," Prance said doubtfully.

"We haven't much choice," Corinne said. "Of course, it is horrible to think of her losing so much money, but at least her life will be spared. She will still have Appleby Court, and ten thousand pounds besides."

"But what if we turn over the money and Susan doesn't come back?" Prance asked. "If there were only some way we could negotiate, tell the bleater he must bring Susan to the forest if he wants the money. How did the note arrive, Luten?"

"Otto was dozing in his study. When he awoke half an hour ago, the note was on his desk. He had left the door to the garden open to catch the breeze. The fellow had the gall to come right into the house." He turned an accusing eye on Corinne. "If someone had been here, watching Otto, she might have caught him."

"I was only gone for an hour," she shot back.

"I hope you didn't expect Corinne to tackle a blood-thirsty kidnapper!" Prance said, bristling in indignation. He put a protective arm around her and pulled her against his side.

157

"She might have seen him, is what I meant. Followed him, or seen which direction he took at least."

"He would hardly have come prancing into the study if I had been there," she said. "He would have chosen some other time when he was sure of not being seen. There is no point blaming me, Luten."

"You're right. It's just nerves," he said, flinging a hand into the air. "You don't have to protect her, Reg. I wasn't planning to strike her."

Prance let her go. Luten began pacing to and fro in the shabby saloon. Corinne noticed that, unlike Coffen and even the dapper Prance, Luten showed not a whit of disarray after his trip. Iridescent rainbows gleamed off his smooth black hair as the sun streamed through the windows. His shirt points were stiff, and his jacket unwrinkled. How did he do it?

Luten interrupted his pacing to say, "What I particularly dislike is the demand that Otto go alone."

"Could one of you not go in his place?" she asked. "So long as the kidnapper gets the money, surely that is all he cares about."

"A disguise!" Prance exclaimed, leaping on the idea. "It would require padding, of course, and the loan of that article Otto calls a hat. Take his rig—as Corinne says, in the dark, who would notice the difference? The kidnapper won't show his face. He'll be hiding somewhere nearby. Does Otto know where this blasted oak is?"

"He says it's near the northern edge of the forest," Luten replied. "It came down in a storm this spring. All the locals know about it. It was one of the oldest trees in the forest."

"But would a stranger know about it? Methinks not," Prance said. "This confirms that the fellow is a local."

Otto came out of his study, smiling in relief. "You heard the news?"

158

"Indeed we have, Otto," Prance said. "We have just been discussing how to handle it. Fear not, we shan't send you alone into the forest."

Otto stared in consternation. "It is for me to go. The note says so. At midnight, alone, with the money in bills. Mrs. Malboeuf brought me a valise to hold the money."

They argued, but Otto was adamant. He felt he was in some way responsible for Susan's abduction, and he would go to rescue her. There was no point arguing with him. He announced that he would have a bath before dinner, and the others must help themselves to wine.

"Where did you put the valise?" Luten asked him.

"Locked in the safe in the study, and the key right here," he said, patting his watch pocket. Then he left.

"At least he is sober," Prance said uncertainly. "Poor fellow. He is treating this transaction as if it were a wedding, or a funeral. I doubt he's had a bath in a month. Such a tremendous undertaking will sober him up."

They were still discussing the delivery of the ransom money an hour later when Coffen returned from the inquest wearing a heavy scowl.

"You're in the soup not showing up to give your testimony, my lad," he said to Prance.

"Egads! I forgot all about it."

"You'd forget your head if it weren't stuck on. I said you was sick and told them about your finding Jeremy's body. They want a written statement, and you have to get it stamped by a JP. I thought you was going to change your duds." He looked at Prance's still wilting shirt points.

"I was," Prance said, thinking of the job of writing up his testimony and getting it stamped.

"Anyhow, it was a dead waste of time," Coffen continued. "The idiot coroner says Jeremy was fatally shot while in the execution of a crime. If Soames was the highwayman, then I'm a Frenchman."

"C'est vous qui le dit," Prance said airily.

"I wish you would quit that babbling in Italian." Coffen scowled. "I spoke to Hodden. You might as well talk to a jug. Tarsome fellow. I've not had a bite for hours. I asked Tobin to bring some tea and bread and butter— Why are you all staring like that? It's hours till dinnertime."

"The ransom note came," Luten said, handing it to him.

Coffen snatched it and perused it quickly for clues. "I've seen this sort of paper before," he said, wrinkling his brow with the effort of thought.

"One sees it everywhere," Prance informed him. "It is about the most common sort of notepaper. In fact, it is the same sort I used for my sketch of Blackmore's dinnerware." He drew out his sketch and compared the papers, which were certainly similar.

"Anyone recognize the writing?" was Coffen's next effort.

Prance sighed. "If you look closely, you will see it is printed, not written, done to disguise the penmanship."

"He writes pretty well, wouldn't you say? Not an illiterate fellow, is what I mean. The spelling and grammar and all that are right, ain't they?"

"It's hardly Shakespeare," Prance said, "but literate, I suppose. Pretty straightforward, with no airs or graces about it."

"Do we know anyone like that?" Coffen asked, pinching his brow.

"You are beating a dead horse, Pattle," Prance said. "The note contains no secret clues. The matter under discussion was how we are to talk Otto into letting one of us go in his stead."

"Why would you want to do that? It'll only get the kidnapper's back up."

"Otto's an old man and so eager to get Susan back that he won't negotiate. If I could go in his place, I would insist that the bounder bring Susan to me before I handed over a penny."

Coffen studied the note again. "He says he will send her home at one o'clock. We can wait one hour. He'll do as he says. Honor among thieves."

"You misunderstand the cliché, Pattle. We are not thieves," Prance declared.

"True." Coffen massaged his ear, then said, "Why don't we follow Otto when he goes?"

"Or better," Luten said, "go before him? Well before, say nightfall, and be there before the kidnapper arrives. If there's more than one of them, we might even overhear where they have Susan and rescue her without handing over the blunt."

Mrs. Malboeuf arrived with a tea tray and slammed it onto the table. When the china and silver had stopped rattling, Luten said with a glare, "Thank you, Mrs. Malboeuf."

Mrs. Malboeuf turned to Corinne. "There's a parcel come for you while you were out, milady. I put it in your bedroom so as you'd find it, in case I forgot to give it to you."

"A parcel for me?" she asked. "I haven't sent for anything. Who knows I'm here?"

"It was left outside the kitchen door. Peggy stumbled over it when she went to the garden for parsley. It might have been there since last night for all I know. I'd fetch it for you, but I have the roast in the oven, haven't I?"

"Send Peggy for it, if you please," Luten said at his most toplofty.

Mrs. Malboeuf snorted, but apparently did as she was told, for Peggy did arrive with the parcel a moment later.

161

Chapter Twenty

While they waited, Corinne poured tea and Coffen snabbled down half a dozen slices of bread and butter.

The parcel had not come through the post. It was just a brown paper bag, with the words "For Lady deCoventry" printed on the outside. Corinne opened the bag and drew out the blue kid reticule that had been stolen from her room two nights before.

"My reticule," she said in bewilderment. "I wish he had sent back my new sprigged muslin and cashmere shawl along with it." She peered into the bag.

"Beggars can't be choosers," Coffen said. "Is your blunt there?"

She drew out her money purse. "Yes, it's all here. I can repay you the money I borrowed for stockings, Prance."

"Oh, do let them be a gift, *cara mia*! I get so few chances to give a lady anything of that sort."

"Pay him," Luten growled.

"Thank you, Prance, I accept," Corinne said, and gave him a kiss on the cheek. She did not look within a right angle of Luten, but she knew that he was scowling at her.

She searched the purse and said, "Now, that is odd! The money is here, but my comb and mirror are gone. That lovely little mirror you gave me, Reggie. My handkerchief is missing."

"Anything else?" Coffen asked.

"Nothing important," she said with a little frown.

"Take a good look. You don't know what might be important," Coffen said.

"I had a little tin box of lemon drops. They're gone. Oh, and a sketch I had cut out of a magazine for a new bonnet."

"Aha! That sounds like a woman's work. Sweets and bonnets, mirror and comb. If it were a man, he'd know enough to leave the rubbish behind and take the blunt."

"The mirror was not rubbish! But it does sound like the work of a woman," Prance agreed.

"Was there ever any doubt that the gown and shawl and silk stockings were taken for a woman?" Luten asked. "There is obviously a female involved. She took what suited her and sent the rest back, probably via her boyfriend."

"But since they're thieves, why didn't they keep my money?" Corinne asked, still rooting through her reticule. "Now, this is *really* strange! There is something here that doesn't belong to me."

"What is it?" Coffen asked eagerly.

"A box of headache powders. Not even the sort I use." She held the box up. Everyone looked at it in confusion.

"Then we're looking for a woman who's prone to headache," Coffen said. "Possibly even with a headache, since she lost her powders in your reticule."

"It is certainly very odd," Luten said, "but we mustn't let it distract us from Susan."

Corinne felt a little sting of anger. Nothing must distract him from Susan! Of course, he was right, but it still hurt to hear him dismiss her little mystery as if it were no more than a nuisance.

"Which of us do you want to go to the forest?" Prance asked, and prayed that he would not be the one selected.

"I'll go myself as soon as it's dark," Luten replied.

"You'll be there for hours," Prance objected. "Eleven o'clock is plenty early enough."

"Well, say ten o'clock," Luten said.

"If you're as fagged as I am after that trip, you'll fall sound asleep," Coffen said. "I could swear the pillow was stuffed with wood chips. It scratched my cheek."

"I'll take a jug of coffee with me to keep awake."

"And a bite to eat," Coffen added. "If your stomach takes to growling, they'll hear you. Give the show away."

"A gentleman's stomach does not growl," Prance decreed. "And a lady, of course, does not have a stomach. Not in company at least."

They soon parted to dress for dinner. Corinne reviewed the strange events of the day as she dressed. The ransom note's arriving so late was odd enough, almost as if it were an afterthought, but oddest of all was the return of her reticule with a few trifles removed and the money still there.

She lifted the lid of the old Spanish chest with the flower carving and looked again at the lingerie stored in it. The unceremonious delivery of the ransom note through the study door suggested that the kidnapper was someone local, someone familiar with the house and the family. Perhaps someone who knew Otto would be asleep or drunk by late afternoon. The return of her purse to the back door also had an air of familiarity to it. Was it a local servant who had done it? It was even possible that Mrs. Malboeuf was involved, and/or her niece, Peggy.

How could she spy on them? There was a curtained arch at the bottom of the servants' stairs, leading to the kitchen. The door had been removed as it knocked against the china cabinet. Corinne glanced at her watch. She had a quarter of an hour before dinner. She hurried

164

along the hall, tiptoed down the dark, narrow staircase, and put her ear to the curtain. Mrs. Malboeuf's trumpeting voice could have been heard through six inches of forged steel.

"How are them potatoes coming along, Peg?" she asked in her gruff voice.

There was the rattle of a lid, then Peggy replied, "Coming along nicely, Auntie. Should I take the meat out of the oven?"

"Best see to the plum preserves. Scoop the top out of the bottle. It's covered in green mold. Make sure you don't get any of it in the bowl."

Corinne's face screwed up in distaste. She'd not touch the plum preserves!

"It's odd about her ladyship's reticule, ain't it?" Peggy said.

"There's plenty of odd things going on in this house, but at least it seems we'll be getting Miss Enderton back. Let us hope this lot go back where they come from and leave us in peace."

"I miss her ever so," Peggy said, and began sniffling.

Well, that didn't sound very guilty. Corinne was about to tiptoe back upstairs when she heard a knock at the kitchen door.

"See who that is," Mrs. Malboeuf said to Peggy.

The door was opened. Peggy said, "Oh, it's you, Judy. How can you get away from the Hall so close to dinnertime?" Corinne assumed it was one of Blackmore's servants. His was the only "Hall" in the immediate neighborhood.

"His lordship don't take dinner till eight. It eats up half the evening. I wish he'd eat at a decent hour like a Christian. I came to see if you've heard anything about Miss Enderton."

"The ransom note came," Peggy said.

"No! How much for?"

"Twenty-five thousand. It'll clean poor Miss Enderton out entirely. It's every penny of her dot."

Corinne listened sharply. Susan actually had thirty-five thousand now, thanks to Otto's wise investing. The kidnapper obviously wasn't aware of it.

"When's it to be delivered?" Judy asked. "Did you hear?"

"Tobin's had his ear to the door. He says midnight, at the blasted oak. Of course, they didn't tell us nothing, but Auntie heard them talking about it and put Tobin on the alert. I'd not go into that forest at midnight for all the tea in China. It wouldn't surprise me none if the poor old gaffer didn't have heart failure. There's a cruel mind behind these doings, Judy."

"Oh, there is and all. We're not safe in our beds. His lordship was at that inquest in town. It seems Jeremy Soames was the highwayman. Can you beat that?"

"If he was the highwayman, then I'm a monkey's aunt," Mrs. Malboeuf said. "He was a gentleman, even if he hadn't two pennies to rub together. Stop your chatter, Peggy. There's work to be done."

"I'm leaving then," Judy said. "I was just worried about poor Miss Enderton. I can't stop thinking of her. It's awful. So awful."

The door squeaked open; presumably Judy exited, for Mrs. Malboeuf said, "I don't see what she's got to sniffle about. It's ourselves that are stuck with all the extra work, to say nothing of his lordship's fancy-pants butler sticking his nose into what don't concern him. He tells me he wants water boiling for coffee at nine-thirty. Now, what the deuce does his lordship want with coffee at such an hour? He'll have had his tea a short while before. He's up to something. Give me that platter for the roast, Peg."

Corinne tiptoed back upstairs, convinced that Mrs.

166

Malboeuf and Peggy were innocent of any complicity in Susan's disappearance, even if they did serve bad preserves.

When she reached the upper landing, Luten was leaving his bedchamber. He had changed for dinner and looked elegant in a black jacket, with an immaculate cravat arranged in intricate tucks. A modest diamond pin sparkled in the folds of linen.

"Don't let that Malboeuf creature impose on you," Luten said sternly. "If you want something, insist that the servants fetch it for you. You shouldn't be using the servants' stairs. What were you after?"

"I was snooping," she said. "It occurred to me that Malboeuf might have something to do with Susan's abduction, but it can't be true. She and Peggy are distraught over it. And so is Judy."

"Judy? Which one is she?"

"She's Blackmore's servant. She dropped in to inquire for Susan."

"Now, that is interesting! Blackmore is sending his snoops into the house, is he?"

"I don't think he even knew she was here."

He took her arm, and they went to the front staircase. "Simon has been keeping his ears open," Luten said. "He also thinks Malboeuf is innocent. This scheme is too ambitious for servants, though someone might have been making use of them."

"I expect you're referring to Blackmore, but I don't think he is responsible either. As he offered for Susan, he must have discussed financial matters with Otto. He knew she has thirty-five thousand, but the ransom demand is only for twenty-five."

"I fancy Blackmore is a little deeper than that. He would know common gossip pegs Susan's dot at

167

twenty-five. To ask for the whole sum would narrow the scope of possible abductors, probably to himself and Soames."

"We seem to be going around in circles," she said. "Just when you think you've got something straight, you hit another curve. But at least we know the ransom note is legitimate, since Susan's ring was with it. She always wore that ring. It belonged to her mama."

Luten frowned. "Yes, she used to wear it on the third finger of her left hand."

"That's the only finger it fit."

"The strange thing is, she wasn't wearing it last February. I noticed she was wearing a little silver ring with clasped hands holding a heart. She wore it on her third finger, left hand."

"Was she? I gave it to her myself. It's Irish. A Claddagh, it is called. Did she not say I had given it to her?"

"No, I would have remembered if she had. Of course, that doesn't mean she had stopped wearing the pearl ring altogether. She wore a silver shawl that evening, so perhaps that is why she chose the silver ring. You might look in her dresser after dinner and see if the Irish ring is there."

"I'll do it this minute!" Corinne exclaimed, and ran back upstairs, with Luten hard at her heels. She was not surprised that Luten had noticed what shawl Susan had been wearing and what ring. He took some interest in ladies' toilettes, but that he should remember it months later seemed strange. As if Susan had been much on his mind. And it was the third finger of her left hand—why had he been paying particular attention to that interesting digit?

They darted to Susan's room, to her dresser, and began

searching through the little box of minor treasures she kept out of the safe for daily wear. The Irish ring wasn't there.

"She wouldn't keep it in the safe," Corinne said. "It wasn't that valuable, just a trinket."

"I'll speak to Otto, but I shan't tell him what we fear."

They rushed back downstairs. Otto opened the safe for them and drew out a small wooden chest with the lid inlaid in nacre and the segmented cavity lined in deep blue velvet. The jewels glimmered like a miniature pirate's treasure chest. The family sapphires were there, the small necklace of diamonds and matching earrings, a ruby and pearl pin, and a few other items, each in its own compartment. The Irish ring was not there.

"Did she usually wear her pearl ring, Otto?" Luten asked.

"I'm pretty sure she did. She was fond of the little hand ring you gave her, Lady deCoventry. She wore it a good deal as well, but I hadn't seen it on her lately. She hadn't lost the pearl ring, or she would have mentioned it. She was likely wearing both of them, one on each hand. She liked baubles."

"Yes, that must be it," Corinne said. Luten merely frowned.

When they had left Otto, she said, "What is bothering you, Luten?"

"I don't like to invent another curve, but . . . might the pearl ring have been stolen the night the intruder was in Susan's room? Was he rummaging around at her toilet table?"

"I believe he was. But . . . are you suggesting that the theft of my gown and reticule and Susan's abduction were both done by the same man?"

"I think I'm suggesting something quite different," he said hesitantly. "That some clever scoundrel decided to steal some personal belonging of Susan's to convince us that he has her. Any of the locals would know no ransom note has been received. He might be exploiting the affair, using the ring to convince us he has her. Being an amateur, he couldn't resist a few other easy pickings while he was about it. Or perhaps he took the reticule and gown to make it look like an ordinary ken smashing."

"Then who *does* have her?"

He shrugged helplessly. "I haven't the faintest idea." He took a crippling grip on her elbow, as if he feared she, too, might disappear, and led her to the saloon.

Chapter Twenty-one

Dinner was a quiet meal. Everyone was wrapped up in his own thoughts. Otto turned his wineglass upside down, indicating his intention to remain sober until Susan was recovered. The others pushed the dry mutton and wet potatoes around their plates and drank lightly. Corinne did take one taste of the plum preserves and noticed a sharp bite indicating they had begun to ferment. After dinner, Otto went into the garden to blow a cloud, perhaps to remove himself from the temptation of the wine decanter.

This was the first opportunity Luten and Corinne had to tell the others of their findings regarding the two rings. They had decided not to trouble Otto with their fear, lest it drive him to drink.

"You have got to tell Otto, Luten," Prance said, after the thing had been discussed. "He might be handing Susan's money over to some opportunist who doesn't have Susan but has only snatched her ring from the dresser. The broadsheets have put the idea into his head that there is real money to be made out of it. Otto will have lost niece and money. It will be the death of him. And what if the real kidnapper makes his demand after the blunt is gone? No, it's too dangerous."

"I was just thinking," Coffen said, "if this demand is a fake, then who *has* got Susan, and why hasn't he come forward? I don't say it's so or think it, but it could even have been Soames. That would account for not getting a ransom note. Since he's dead, you see. And likely Susan is, too, by now. Starved to death, poor child."

"But what if the note is genuine?" Corinne said. "Can we risk not taking the money and possibly cause her death?"

"What we've got to do is follow the oiler," Coffen said. "You go on ahead at ten as you planned, Luten. Me and Prance will be lurking about, one on either side of the road to follow the scoundrel when he comes out of the forest. Cosh him on the head, steal the money back, force him to lead us to Susan."

"The man is not a fool. He will have thought of that and taken precautions," Prance said.

"Dash it, what precautions can he take? He can't fly away from the forest. We'd ought to get Hodden in on it as well. Form a circle around the whole forest."

"He'll disappear into the trees," Prance said. "Hide the money in a hole somewhere and come back for it later. I daresay the woods are full of poachers. We won't know which man is the kidnapper."

"I'll know," Luten said. "I won't let him out of my sight."

"Then you had best have a mount tethered nearby," Corinne said. "He'll be mounted for a fast getaway."

"I hadn't planned to walk to the forest. It's a few miles away," Luten replied. "Coffen's idea of lurking outside the forest but nearby is not a bad one. We don't know how many of them are in on it. It could be a whole gang, but I doubt more than one or two will come to pick up the money. If you see them come out of the forest, follow them. If they disappear into it, I shall follow, with my pistol charged and ready to fire. One way or the other, we'll get him—or them, as the case may be."

172

Country hours were kept at Appleby Court. It was still only eight-thirty, with time to kill before leaving. Prance decided to pay a call on Blackmore, to taunt him about Mrs. Spencer, née Prissy Trueheart. He had doodled up a new design for the dinnerware featuring a satyr in lieu of the lion, with petticoats flouncing all around it. "All in jest," he said.

"Be sure you're back before ten," Coffen said.

"Probably by nine," Prance replied, laughing. "I doubt he will welcome me with open arms, but I cannot resist my little gibe."

Luten was pacing back and forth. "I'd best change," he said, and left to speak to his valet.

"What will you be doing while we're gone?" Coffen asked Corinne.

"Waiting and worrying. What else can I do?"

"You could say a few prayers."

"That, too."

"I have a little errand to run myself."

"What's that?" she asked, with only mild interest.

"Bloodhounds. There's a fellow near East Grinstead—Lafferty—who has a couple of dandy ones. Hodden used them early on, but he could get no trace of Susan. I'll see if Lafferty will lend them to me. I didn't mention it to Luten. He'd only worry about their barking and giving the show away."

"They probably would."

"Lafferty says he's trained 'em to silence, but I'll muzzle 'em. Shan't be long. If Luten's looking for me, tell him . . . tell him I went out for a walk."

Corinne was left alone, with a foretaste of the long evening to come. She foresaw a hundred possibilities for this scheme to go wrong. What if the men knocked Luten out and disappeared into the depths of the forest with the money? What if Susan wasn't returned after? Or what if

173

she returned and had been violated? Beaten, raped—anything was possible.

To escape her thoughts, and to make sure that Otto wasn't drinking, she went to his study and began a game of chess with him. He was the better player, but he was so distraught that neither of them made a good showing. When she heard the front door open, she used it as an excuse to abandon the game. Otto showed no interest in drink that evening. He had had the temptation removed from his study.

She went to see who had returned. It was Prance. He looked somewhat crestfallen.

"He had already found out about Prissy and given her her congé," he said. "Lord Henry Dalyrymple, an aging roué who used to spend a deal of time at the theaters, saw her on the High Street yesterday. He called on Blackmore and mentioned seeing Prissy Trueheart. Blackmore was not tardy to put two and two together. She's left East Grinstead, gone back to London to try her luck there. She had conned Blackmore entirely. He thought she was a respectable married lady whose husband had run off to London and left her penniless. Well, relatively respectable. Certainly not a prostitute and a known thief. He asked me to keep his secret. Of course, I shall, except to you, *cara mia*. I have no secrets from you."

Corinne could dredge up very little interest in Prissy Trueheart. "That's too bad," she said. "I wonder if Coffen asked Hodden to search her cottage. He mentioned it."

"Hodden refused. So far as he's concerned, the highwayman case is closed. I didn't show Blackmore the satyr design for the dinnerware. He was heartbroken. He actually loved the wench. I abandoned him to his brandy and left him decently alone. It is all one can do in these cases. A broken heart must mend itself."

174

"You'll want to change before you go to the forest," she said. "That's a new jacket, isn't it?"

"It is, but the left sleeve is poorly set in. It pulls when I raise my arm. I am hoping to ruin it beyond repair tonight. One hates just to throw away a good jacket, but really, it annoys me dreadfully every time I put it on. Even Weston is only human. Who would have thought it? I shall change my trousers and put on top boots, however. One does not ride in evening slippers."

He pointed the dainty toe of his slipper, admired it a moment, then rose and went abovestairs to make his toilette. Luten came down, dressed in a blue jacket, buckskins, and top boots, and went into Otto's office. Coffen returned a little later.

"Did you get the bloodhounds?" Corinne asked.

"Lafferty had hired them out to some other fellow. He was expecting them back at any moment, but I couldn't wait any longer. He's to send them along as soon as they come."

Prance returned to the saloon at nine forty-five, outfitted in the black evening jacket, buckskins, and top boots.

"If anyone should see me like this, I would never hold up my head again," he said, though he actually thought it looked rather well.

A moment later, Luten appeared at the door, carrying his insulated bottle of coffee, with a pistol bulging in his pocket. Luten, Prance, and Coffen held a hurried conversation.

"I think one of you should follow Otto," Luten said. "Don't let him out of your sight. It's possible he'll be held up on his way to the forest. The scoundrel knows he'll be carrying twenty-five thousand pounds. Prance, you'll do it?"

"Of course."

175

"And you, Coffen," Luten continued, "you come with me, but find some hiding spot on the outer edge of the forest."

"I thought I'd go along a little later," Coffen said.

"We might as well go together."

"I don't have any coffee."

Luten rolled his eyes ceilingward. "You can take mine."

Corinne knew Coffen was waiting for the bloodhounds and said, "Why don't you go along now, Luten, and I'll have some coffee made for Coffen. He'll leave very soon."

"Very well, but don't get lost." He gave Corinne a questioning look. She sensed that he wanted a private word with her and used the coffee as an excuse to accompany him to the front door. When the order had been given and they were in the privacy of the hall, Luten set his coffee bottle on the side table and seized her hands in his.

"Well, this is it," he said. "With luck, we'll have Susan and the money back tonight, and we can get on with . . ."

"Go back to London, you mean?"

"I meant get on with our own lives."

"Yes," she said uncertainly.

"Aren't you going to wish me luck?"

"Of course. Good luck, Luten."

His fingers nudged up her arms. "That is not what I meant." His head descended, and his lips brushed hers. Suddenly his arms were around her, crushing her against him.

The amorous attack came like a bolt out of the blue. Corinne was half-convinced Luten was in love with Susan, even that he had offered for her again last February. Doubt hindered her response. She put her arms on his shoulders and pushed him off.

176

"You—we shouldn't be doing this," she said stiffly.

He looked around the empty hall. "There's no one to see," he pointed out.

"Surely that's not the only thing that matters!"

"Dammit, we're practically engaged. If it hadn't been for Susan, we would be by now."

Her heart jumped into her throat. "What do you mean? What are you talking about?"

"You know what I mean. We'll discuss it later. Now, kiss me, dammit."

Without waiting, he pulled her back into his arms and kissed her soundly. The imminent danger lent a poignant edge to the embrace. He kissed her as if he feared he would never have another chance. His lips burned on hers, while his arms riveted her to him, until she no longer doubted it was she and no one else whom he loved. She felt it in every atom of her being. Whatever was going on between Luten and Susan, it wasn't what she feared. When the embrace was over, he held her at arm's length and smiled wanly.

"It's been a hell of a visit, hasn't it?" he said. Then he put on his curled beaver, picked up the coffee, gave her a peck on the cheek, and went out the door.

She waited a moment to collect her thoughts before returning to the saloon. Glancing in the mirror, she saw the moonish smile on her face and schooled her expression to indifference. But her heart was light. She couldn't quell the happiness in her eyes. She thought of Susan and managed a suitable face, or thought she had.

Prance scrutinized her and said, "I have been wanting to run upstairs and change. I have decided after all that I cannot appear in such a mixed ensemble, even if there will be no one but felons to see me. I shall see myself. Lucullus dining with Lucullus, you know." She obviously didn't know what he was talking about, or care. "I only waited as I feared to interrupt the lovemaking. If you tell me that wretch has come up to scratch *now*, after not doing it in time for my party, I shall— Well, don't expect another party from me, Countess. I hope you noticed I called you 'Countess.' I am very vexed with you."

"We're not engaged," she said. "You will be the first to know when—if that happens."

"I heard that *when*, sly puss!"

He flounced out of the room and went upstairs to change his jacket.

Coffen squeezed his forehead up like a washboard and said, "I hope them bloodhounds get here before I have to leave."

"Are they really necessary?"

"We were fools not to have thought of them before."

"They would only have run in circles. Susan's scent would be all over the park."

"That's as may be, but the kidnappers' scent won't be."

"You need something that belongs to the person you want to find, a scent for the dogs to follow."

"I know that. I'm going to set it up with Otto now, douse the corners of the valise with vanilla, pour a bit on my own hankie to let the hounds sniff, so they'll know what smell they're after."

"I doubt it will work," she said.

"I don't see why not. Why, vanilla smells so strong I might be able to follow the smell myself."

Coffen went and was gone for some time. When he returned, he said, "It's done."

"I can smell the vanilla from here," she replied.

Tobin came with the bottle of coffee and left.

"Still no dogs. What should I do?" Coffen asked. "I don't suppose you'd care to bring the dogs along for me when they get here?"

178

"I can't go alone!"

"You wouldn't be alone. You'd have two big dogs. Safe as a church. I figured you'd be sneaking out to follow us anyhow, or I wouldn't ask you."

Corinne wondered why she hadn't planned to follow them. She hated being left out of things. Was it only because she had been angry with Luten? That must be it, for she was suddenly very eager to be part of the excitement.

"All right. I'll do it."

"Good girl. Well, I'm off, then."

Corinne still had plenty of time to kill. Prance and Otto were not leaving until eleven-thirty. She had a private word with the butler about the bloodhounds. When they came, they were to be hidden behind the stable and brought to the front door with Susan's mount after Otto had left. Tobin looked askance, but he didn't ask any questions. He knew dire doings were afoot and preferred not to know too much, lest Hodden pay a call in the morning.

When Prance and Otto left, she was alone. She ran up and changed into Susan's too small riding habit. When she came down, Tobin told her the bloodhounds had arrived and were waiting outside, along with the mount.

"Thank you, Tobin," she said, and sailed out the front door, into the dark silence of the night.

Chapter Twenty-two

The air was cool, the waxing moon bright above, but a mist hung over the ground in low-lying areas when Luten left Appleby. Ashdown Forest was due south. Moonlight and mist silvered the bushes that grew along the road. No one else was out, not a carriage, not a gig, a mounted rider, or even a pedestrian. He had the road to himself. He cantered along at a fast pace, eager to reach his destination and get the lay of the land. After a quarter of an hour's ride, the edge of the forest loomed in the distance, a black cloud, blurred by fog.

Otto had given him directions to the blasted oak. One entered the forest road, and then left the road after a hundred yards, turning left. Luten had not thought it would be so dark. The fog was thicker here, and the trees met overhead, robbing the forest of moonlight. He decided to tether his mount on the right side of the roadway, well hidden by trees and well away from the blasted oak.

When this was done, he returned to the road and quietly picked his way through the forest, looking left and right for the blasted oak. It was nowhere to be seen. He forged on, taking little side trips to left and right, being scratched by thorn bushes and barking his shins and once being poked in the eye by the pointed end of a bare branch.

It was ten minutes before he found the blasted oak.

There was no mistaking it. Its diameter was over a yard, and the leaves on its branches were still unwithered. He peered into the mist for a hiding spot that would let him see Otto and the kidnapper without being detected. The fog dictated that he be close to the tree. He chose an elm whose trunk was wide enough to hide him and took up his position. With a couple of hours to wait, he decided to sit down. It was demmed uncomfortable on the damp earth. He should have brought the horse blanket. He'd had such trouble finding the spot that he was reluctant to leave it to get the blanket.

He tried to get comfortable. As he became accustomed to the quiet, he began to notice small sounds. The whisper of leaves overhead as the wind stirred through the branches, the occasional rustle of marauding night creatures in the undergrowth. Time passed slowly. He was sure he had been there an hour. When he drew out his watch, he discovered to his consternation that he couldn't read it in the darkness. Had he been here an hour? Perhaps it was only half an hour. There was no way of telling. He thought of Susan, and Corinne, and of the many things that might go wrong with this night's work.

When his muscles became cramped, he rose and stretched his limbs. He heard a shot in the distance, so far away he assumed it was poachers. They must have eyes like owls to spot their prey in this fog. He decided to have a cup of coffee to pass the time. Simon had flavored it just as he liked, no cream, but plenty of sugar. It wasn't as good as his own coffee. Malboeuf must use some inferior sort. She would. How did Susan put up with the slovenly creature?

Yet with all her faults, she was apparently faithful to her mistress, according to Simon. And according to Corinne as well. His thoughts turned more happily to Corinne. He rested his head on his chest and sat, daydreaming.

Suddenly he felt very tired. He rose to shake off the lethargy and found that his legs couldn't hold him. He stumbled, clinging to the tree, and fell to the ground. His last thought was that the coffee had been drugged. Who . . . ?

The most nervous man on the prowl that night, with the possible exception of the kidnapper, was Sir Reginald Prance. Violence had its place in the world, and that place, so far as he was concerned, was the stage of a theater. He enjoyed watching a good theatrical sword fight. As to the current craze for bruisers! He had never set foot in Jackson's Boxing Parlour and never intended to. He did not attend boxing events, cockfights, or any other sort of senseless cruelty. Most particularly, he avoided physical confrontations himself.

He did care for his reputation, however. He could not refuse to follow Otto to the forest and keep an eye on him, but he did hope and pray that the kidnapper would be true to his word and wait until Otto had passed under the care of Luten before showing his face—or mask. Of course, he would be masked. Prance's mind strayed to the masks of Greek drama, and from there it flitted to a dozen other passing thoughts.

He rode several yards behind Otto, losing sight of him at an occasional bend in the road, but always keeping his ears wide open, ready to rush forward at the first ominous sound. When he heard the telltale clip-clop of a horse on the road behind him, he jerked to attention. He became extremely nervous. He drew out his pistol, wondering if he would have the pluck to use it. The rider behind him did not seem intent on overtaking him, however. The desultory gait of the animal—just one, wasn't it?—sounded like a mule. Still, he was relieved when the rider turned in at one of the farms along the road.

Prance kept a steady pace. When he saw the dark out-line of the forest ahead, he drew a great sigh of relief. There! There was Otto riding his gig into the forest. Prance rode closer until he was at the edge of the tree line, then he found concealment in the shadow of a tall elm. Coffen should be here by now. He had left over an hour ago. Prance heard a rustle behind him and leapt a foot from his saddle.

"It's only me," Coffen said softly. "Nothing going on here. The kidnapper hasn't come yet."

Prance was so relieved to have human company (and a helping hand in case of trouble) that he actually smiled at Coffen. "You saw Otto going in?"

"I did. The kidnapper hasn't come yet. I wonder how long we'll have to wait for him to show up, or if he'll even come this way. More likely to slip up behind Otto through the trees, I should think. I wonder what time it is. I hope I get my watch back from the scoundrel. He might have sold it by now."

"It must be close to midnight."

"Yes."

They waited, Coffen on foot, Prance seated on his mount, both listening, peering down the road and into the dense darkness of the forest. Coffen decided he should get on his horse, too, in case a chase was involved. Nei-ther of them heard the kidnapper's stealthy track through the forest. The man was waiting at the blasted oak for Marchbank. Otto spoke quietly when he handed over the valise.

"Where is she? Is she safe?" he asked.

The masked man nodded, then said in a gruff voice, "She'll be home at one o'clock, as promised. Don't worry, sir. She's perfectly safe."

Then he took the valise, hefted it but didn't even look inside, and vanished on foot. His horse was waiting deeper in the woods. Otto heard a gentle whinny, followed by hoofbeats. Just one horse. He looked around and called softly, "Luten! Luten, are you there?"

Since the kidnapper had come alone, Otto expected that Luten would leap out at him with his pistol in his hand and demand the money back, unmask him, and reveal the face of evil. Where was Luten? Otto called again and paced forward, looking past the trees, where the mist was a great impediment to seeing. After a few moments he gave up. His gig was waiting by the side of the road. He climbed in, turned the horse around, and headed out of the forest.

Prance waited a moment to make sure Otto wasn't being followed, then cantered forward, followed by Coffen.

"What happened?" Coffen demanded. "How many men were there? Did Luten catch the bounder?"

Otto drew to a stop. "Only one man, on foot, with a horse nearby. I saw no sign of Luten."

"The man got away with the money?" Prance asked.

Otto lifted his hands helplessly. "I gave him the money. He left. He says Susan is safe, she'll be home as promised. I didn't hear Luten follow him. There might have been more than one man. Perhaps the accomplice discovered Luten hiding and knocked him out. So long as he sends Susan home safely . . ."

"This is a fine how-do-you-do." Coffen scowled. "While we sat with our hands in our pockets, patting ourselves on the back for doing our bit, they went and got Luten. We'd best go in and search for him, Prance."

Otto frowned and said, "Surely they wouldn't have harmed him."

"Perhaps they've kidnapped him," Prance suggested, and giggled nervously. "Come along, Pattle. You go on home, Otto. You will want to be there to greet your niece."

Otto jiggled the reins, and the gig moved forward. Coffen looked down the road. Seeing no sign of Corinne and the bloodhounds, he went into the forest with Prance.

"Luten planned to hide close to the blasted oak," Coffen said. "We'll start there." He looked around in confusion. "That giant oak used to stand out a mile. It's hard finding a tree that ain't there. It was that way, I believe."

They rode toward the meeting spot, Coffen in the lead, as the trees were too dense to ride abreast. When they found the blasted oak, they began to look around, behind nearby trees. It was Coffen who made the discovery.

"I've found him!" he shouted, and leaned down to ascertain that the body was only unconscious, not dead. The deep breaths were regular. "I do believe he's foxed!"

"Luten disguised at such a crucial juncture? I don't believe it. You're overwrought with excitement."

"I'm underwrought if anything."

They felt for a bump on the head and for possible bloodstains. Prance noticed the bottle of coffee, still half-full, and held it up to show Coffen. "It can't be a sleeping draft. Simon made the coffee."

Coffen tilted the bottle and tasted the dregs. "You're basically right, but you're dead wrong. The coffee *is* drugged. Simon made it, but Malboeuf boiled the water, I expect."

"We'll have to get him home. I wonder where he tied his mount."

"I'll have a look about," Coffen said, and stomped through the trees, whistling and calling. Luten's mount whinnied a welcome at the familiar sound. Coffen followed the sound across the road and into the trees and eventually led the mount forward.

It proved extremely difficult to get Luten's inert body over the saddle, especially with Coffen handling the legs.

"Dash it, Pattle, we're not trying to get his feet in the stirrups. We'll have to hang him over the horse's back like a sack of oats."

"Luten won't like it."

"Would he prefer that we leave him here?"

After a frowning pause, Coffen said, "I shouldn't think so, no."

"It is not necessary to answer rhetorical questions."

"Then why do you bother asking them? There, that ought to do it." He picked up Luten's hat, found it refused to remain on Luten's head when the head was hanging down to the ground, put the hat on top of his own, and led the mount out of the forest.

As they came out onto the main road, Coffen saw Corinne, with the leashed bloodhounds running before her.

Prance, who was unaware that Coffen had hired the dogs, said, "Corinne! What on earth—"

"Lafferty's bloodhounds," Coffen said. "A bit late, I fear. Still, better late than never."

Corinne recognized the body hung over the saddle and leapt down. "Luten! What happened to him? Is he hurt? He's not—" A strangled gasp choked the words to silence.

"We think there was laudanum in his coffee," Coffen said. "Mine was all right."

She tried to cradle Luten's head in her arms, murmuring sympathy and encouragement, but it was difficult. "You're sure he's just drugged?"

"His breathing is steady. Deep, but steady," Prance assured her.

"Can't we sit him up properly? This is so ... demeaning."

"Dear girl, if you are implying that I should hold a dead weight of thirteen stone while riding through the fog in the dead of night—well, we would both end up in the ditch," Prance sniffed.

"Oh, very well, but let us get him home before he wakes up."

Coffen had seized the ropes holding the bloodhounds. "I'll just get the lads to work," he said.

Prance shook his head. "It may come as news to you, Pattle, but bloodhounds require a scent to follow."

Coffen waved a handkerchief under their noses. "That's why I doused the corners of the valise with vanilla," he said.

Prance pouted. "Oh. Well done," he said grudgingly. "And do you mean to go alone to confront the kidnappers?"

"There's only one. Otto said so."

Prance looked from Luten's inert body to Corinne to Coffen. "I really should go with Pattle," he said. "What comes first—courtesy, as in accompanying a lady at night, or common sense?"

"Common sense," she said. "You go with Coffen. I'll get Luten home."

"I don't envy you your job—when he awakens," Prance said, and laughed. "He will be in a rare pelter."

Chapter Twenty-three

"You *lost* it!" Susan exclaimed. "You lost my twenty-five thousand pounds! Oh, Rufus, how *could* you!" Tears brimmed in her blue eyes and splashed down over her rose-petal cheeks.

"Dash it, I never wanted to send the note. You are the one who insisted."

The conversation took place on the back doorstep of Greenleigh, where Susan had been awaiting his return. She wore Rufus's greatcoat over a blue-and-white muslin gown. The coat was noticeably too big for her; the gown was soiled and wrinkled.

"What else could we do when Corinne told you they were all wondering why no ransom had been demanded?" Susan asked. "You are the one who said it was cruel to make Otto suffer. Besides, I think Luten was suspicious. Why else did he call twice at Greenleigh? He would have searched your house before long. What would you have said when he found me in your attic?"

"I wish I were dead." Rufus moaned and held his head in his hands.

He felt something warm and hot on his fingers. When he looked at it, he saw it was blood. Susan saw it, too.

"Oh, Rufus, you're hurt!"

"I told you, the man coshed me with the butt of his

pistol after he snatched the valise, to stop me from following him."

"How did he know about the meeting with Otto?" she asked, gnawing her lip. "If I had not told Peggy to put a good strong dose of laudanum in Luten's coffee, I would think it was Luten who had taken the money. It would be just like him," she said testily.

"It might have been Luten for all I know. The fellow was wearing a mask. But what's to do now, Susan? No one knows I collected the money. You can just go on home and say nothing. They'll think the kidnapper got away with your fortune. No one need know what a pair of greenheads we are."

"You're the greenhead! You should have insisted on marrying me at once after I went to all the bother of spending the night under your bachelor roof."

"Dash it, I didn't even know you were there, in my attic. That's gratitude for you, after I went scrambling into your house to get you clean clothes."

"And got the wrong ones," she reminded him. "Corinne is much larger than I."

"I put her reticule back," he said apologetically. "Come, we must go. Otto will be worried. He looked like death when I met him in Ashdown Forest."

"But where shall I say I have been all this time?"

"You were kept blindfolded the whole time. You don't know where you were."

"In a horrid cold barn," she invented. "Shivering and fed on bread and water."

"To say nothing of pounds of sugarplums and honey cake and those lemon drops you stole out of Lady deCoventry's reticule."

She adopted a moue and took his hand. "Don't be angry with me, Rufus. I only did it so you would stop being so proud and stupid and *have* to marry me. I am

189

practically penniless now," she said, peering to see if he was weakening.

"I wish we had gone for the whole thirty-five thousand while we were about it. Then I could marry you."

"They would have suspected it was me if I'd asked for thirty-five. Everyone thinks my dot is only twenty-five. Ten thousand is not much," she said. "And you own Greenleigh. It's not as though you are a fortune hunter, after all. Come with me, Rufus. I cannot face it alone. I shall say I was dumped at your doorstep and called on you for help. They'll believe that. Your house is right on the main road."

"How shall I account for this lump on my head?"

"Smooth your hair over it. No one will notice. Come with me, Rufus," she wheedled, batting her eyelashes shamelessly.

Rufus was no match for her. "I had better do it, or you will pitch yourself into some other imbroglio. Hussy." The last word was a caress.

She took his hand and led him through the park to Appleby Court.

Luten did not awaken from his slumber until Tobin and Simon had got him onto the sofa, fanned his brow, and sprinkled him with cold water. When he opened his eyes, he smelled the pungent odor of burning feathers that Corinne had used in an effort to revive him. A glass of brandy was held to his lips by a black-haired sorceress who gradually took on the lineaments of Lady deCoventry. The dim saloon of Appleby Court was draped in shadows. He saw another form hovering nearby, but did not recognize Otto at first.

"Where am I?" he asked in a faint voice.

"Home safe, Luten," Corinne said, and smoothed the wrinkles from his brow with cool, gentle fingers.

190

He wanted just to lie there, luxuriating in her tender touch and the loving sympathy in her dulcet voice. But something nagged at him. He sat up, shaking his head and looking around. "Susan! The money—"

"You had best drink this," she said, urging the brandy on him.

"They got away with the money," he said in a hollow voice. "What happened?"

"We think there was laudanum in the coffee you took with you," she said.

"Impossible! Simon made that coffee for me."

"Well, the laudanum didn't get into the coffee by itself, and Simon didn't put it there either."

"Malboeuf!"

"There hasn't been time to look into it. I cannot believe she . . ." Yet who else could have done it? "I don't know," she said in confusion.

"What time is it?" He drew out his watch. "Five to one. Susan hasn't come back?"

"Not yet," Otto said. He held his watch in his hand. His eyes only left it to travel to the door into the front hall.

"Where are Coffen and Prance?" Luten asked.

"Following the kidnappers," Corinne replied.

Otto went to the window, lifted back the curtains, and peered into the misty darkness.

"Did the kidnappers have much of a head start?" Luten asked.

"There was only one. About ten minutes, I think," she replied.

"They'll never catch him."

"Coffen had bloodhounds," she said vaguely, not mentioning her own part in the matter.

"I should go and help them."

"We have no idea where they are."

Before more could be said, Otto cried out in joyous

191

accents, "She's back! Susan is back!" He raced into the hall and flung open the front door.

Within seconds, Susan came in, leaning heavily on Rufus's arm, while Otto held on to her hand. Tears fell shamelessly from his aged and rheumy eyes.

"I believe I shall have a glass of wine now to celebrate," he said after a moment. He poured himself a large glass and nearly emptied it in one thirsty gulp. "Sit down, poor child, and tell us all about it."

Susan allowed herself to be seated on the sofa. She immediately put her face in her hands and began sobbing. "It was horrid, Uncle. A horrid ordeal."

He sat down beside her and patted her shoulder. "Poor baby," he crooned. "Poor child. It is all over now. There, dry your eyes, my dear. You are home safe. Nothing else matters."

"Did you get a look at him?" Luten asked her.

"No, I was blindfolded the whole time," she said.

"How many of them were there?"

"One. I only saw—heard one."

"Any notion where you were kept?"

"In a barn. It was dreadfully cold. I had to sleep on the ground, with only a bit of smelly straw for a mattress. I was kept alive on bread and water."

Luten noticed she looked remarkably robust after her prolonged diet of bread and water. When Otto tenderly removed the greatcoat from her shoulders, her gown showed no sign of hay or earth, or such dirt as might be picked up in a barn. It was dusty, and the front stained with food. Not the sort of stains bread and water would leave. They looked like gravy, and perhaps tea or wine. Now, why the deuce was she bamming them?

"How far away was the barn?" he asked.

"I don't know, Luten. I was blindfolded," she said.

192

"How long did it take you to get there? Half an hour, an hour, a day?"

"A few hours, it seemed like. It was hard to tell when I was blindfolded."

"Did he take you in a carriage?"

She hesitated a guilty length of time. "In a farm cart, with a blanket over me," she said.

"Why didn't you jump out? Were you tied?"

"Of course I was tied up," she said angrily.

"Did you drive through East Grinstead?"

"How should I know?"

"The fair was on that day. You would have heard the noise. Or did he plug your ears as well?" he asked satirically.

"He . . . I was doped," she said.

"Luten!" Otto objected. "Have mercy on the poor child."

Susan put her hand in her pocket and drew out a handkerchief to wipe her eyes and to give her time to think. She might have known Luten would be horrid!

Corinne was also having doubts at this unlikely story. She glanced at the handkerchief, then looked again. The tatting along the edge looked familiar—like one of the set Mrs. Ballard had made for her for her birthday. She handed Susan her own fresh handkerchief and took the mussed one from her fingers. She examined it and ascertained that it was one of her own. It must have been taken from her purse, along with her comb and mirror and lemon drops. Susan was fond of sweets. The sugarplums Rufus had bought in town and pretended were for Sally's birthday, the honey cake Rufus pretended he had eaten . . . Susan had been at Rufus Stockwell's house the whole time! And Rufus knew it!

She looked to Rufus and saw his brow was pleated in worry. He was pale and looked exceedingly uncomfort-

193

able. Luten was still pestering Susan with questions. Otto was clucking his objection.

"Do leave the poor child be, Luten," she said. "Let her rest and recover her wits. I would like a word with you in Otto's study. Perhaps you would join us, Mr. Stockwell?"

She gave Luten a commanding look. He knew she was on to something and went with her. Stockwell tagged along, with all the enthusiasm of a man on his way to the tooth drawer.

In the study, Corinne said to Stockwell, "Now, let us have the real story, if you please. We know Susan has been in your attic all the while. Did you kidnap her, or—as I suspect—did she sneak in when you were not looking?"

Rufus lifted his chin and said firmly, "I kidnapped her."

"But you were at the fair when she disappeared," she said. "Cut line, Mr. Stockwell. The truth will out. Let us have it with no bark on."

He met her gaze for a moment, then his eyes fell and his shoulders sagged. "Susan has been pest—hinting that she would like to marry me," he said. "I told her it would not do. The disparity in our fortunes . . . She got into the attic without anyone seeing her while I was at the fair. I knew nothing of it until dawn the next morning, when she crept down while I was still in bed. I was horrified! I didn't know what to do. If anyone found out, she would be ruined. She refused to go home. I couldn't let her starve. I had to feed her, and it was not easy, for I didn't want Mrs. Dorman to know she was there."

"How very unpleasant for you," Corinne said, with every sign of sympathy. "And then what did you do?"

"My hope was that I could convince her to go home and pretend she had been injured, lying in a ditch. But she refused to budge. She is a lady—how could I use

194

physical force? It was the deuce of a dilemma. Then you came to call, and I realized how worried Otto was—all of you, her friends. You mentioned, later, that he was afraid she was dead, since no ransom note had come. It seemed cruel to leave him suffering, so we decided we would pretend she had been kidnapped and sent the note. Just as a way of getting her home, you see. I had finally convinced her we couldn't marry. It was her own money, so it did not really seem so bad."

Luten breathed a sigh of relief. "So you have the money!"

Rufus cast a fearful eye on his inquisitors. "Not exactly," he said. "Peggy came over to tell Sally about the ransom meeting, and how you, Lord Luten, planned to be there, hiding. Sally told me about it. I had a word with Susan, and we decided to take Sally and Peggy into our confidence, as they are both fond of Susan and we knew they would help us. It was arranged that Peggy would slip some laudanum into the water for your coffee. I'm sorry."

Luten glared but held his tongue.

Rufus drew a deep breath and forged ahead with his story. "I'm afraid it gets worse. I collected the valise as arranged in the note. We meant to hide it in some barn or tree and pretend we had found it in a day or two."

"What happened to the money?" Luten asked in a hollow voice.

"It was stolen by the highwayman," Rufus said. "I came out of the forest with the bag tied to my saddle. I didn't use the main road but went in by a little side path the poachers use. The highwayman came out of nowhere. He'd been waiting for me, I swear. Perhaps he followed me from Greenleigh, though I don't see how he could know I was involved. More likely he was lurking about at the blasted oak and got out of the forest by a shorter route. In any case, he pointed a pistol at me and demanded the money. I had to give it to him. I hoped to follow him and get it back, but he ordered me to turn around and hit me over the back of my head with his pistol. I was out cold. When I woke up, I was on the ground." He put his fingers to his head. They came away smeared with blood. "There, you see, that proves it. I am really extremely sorry." He looked ready to burst into tears.

Corinne took pity on him and said, "Of course you are, Mr. Stockwell. You must get that wound looked at."

Luten let off an extremely proficient stream of oaths. Having vented his anger, he said, "The bloodhounds! Let us hope they do the trick."

"Bloodhounds?" Rufus said.

Corinne explained about Lafferty's bloodhounds and the vanilla.

"Oh, I thought the valise had a nice smell," he said. Then he cast a chastened look at Luten. "I know I've been a wretched fool, but I am indeed sorry, milord. What should I do?"

"You have two options, Stockwell. You may marry Miss Enderton, or meet me in the court of twelve paces. It is entirely up to you." Then he strode out of the room to call for his mount.

Rufus said uncertainly, "Is he serious? Does he think I should marry Susan?"

"Oh, indeed, I think you must, Mr. Stockwell. Luten is an excellent shot. You don't want Susan to have to bury you." She tore out of the room after Luten.

Rufus sat down and drew a deep sigh of relief, which fast rose to delight. Then he went to join Susan in the saloon to tell her the good news. Otto was nearly as joyful as Susan.

"Now, if only we could get your money back," he said, shaking his head and reaching for the wine bottle.

Chapter Twenty-four

"Where are you going, Luten?" Corinne demanded. "What are you going to do? I want to go with you."

As the words left her mouth, the door closed behind him. He didn't even bother to say she couldn't accompany him. Despite his great hurry, he had no real idea where he was going. With luck, Pattle's bloodhounds would take up the trail, but which direction had the thief taken? He thought of what Stockwell had said, that the highwayman must have followed him from the forest, as he was waiting for him when he came out. Who knew about the transaction besides the people at Appleby Court and Greenleigh? Blackmore's servant had visited Peggy. Once a servant knew something, the household knew, and from there, it was not long before it was all over the parish.

Luten hopped on his mount and headed, *ventre à terre*, to Blackmore's stable. A stableboy came out.

"I have to see Lord Blackmore, urgently," Luten said.

"Sorry, your lordship, he ain't at home tonight."

"At Mrs. Spencer's, is he?"

The stableboy looked worried. "That ain't for me to say, your lordship."

"It's all right, lad. I know about his mistress."

The boy grinned. "In that case, you might find him there."

Prance had said Prissy Trueheart went back to London, but the servants might not know it yet. She made a good excuse to leave home at night in any case. Her house would be standing empty. A good place to hide the ransom money. No doubt the lease was in Blackmore's pocket.

Thinking of the highwayman, it occurred to Luten that visiting the *soi-disant* Mrs. Spencer would have made a good excuse for late evening absences from home, while Blackmore held up carriages on the highway. Why had Blackmore taken up with the wench? He would certainly know a light-skirt from a lady, whatever act he had put on for Prance. But Blackmore couldn't be the highwayman. He had been under Luten's own observation the night the Turner ladies were held up.

Neither Luten nor anyone who knew Soames believed he was the highwayman. A second thought told Luten it was likely the real highwayman had stolen the ransom money. The next question was, where had he taken it? He would know the shepherd's hut was safe, now that Hodden thought the highwayman was dead. Luten headed for it, taking the shortcut through Blackmore's meadow.

The bloodhounds soon took up the scent and set out through the forest at a great rate, picking a path through the trees, with Coffen and Prance following. All went exceedingly well until they came to a clearing in the forest, at which point the dogs went mad. They began tearing around in circles, yelping their heads off.

Coffen decided he'd best stop and see what had set them off. One of them was pawing at an old box. With his luck, it would be a box that had held vanilla beans, left abandoned.

"It's the valise!" Prance exclaimed. "Is the money in

198

it?" They both hopped down and ran to retrieve the valise.

"Empty," Coffen said, pulling it from the dog's mouth and shaking it upside down. The larger of the blood-hounds thought it a game and leapt into the air, snapping at it. "Watch it, Caesar! That's my fingers you're nipping."

Nero, the other hound, was running in circles. The ropes holding the two became entwined.

"What ails the cur?" Prance asked. "He acts mad. He's got something between his teeth. What is it?"

"I'll be dashed if I'll try to get it from him. Caesar has already taken a bite out of me."

Prance went up to the hound, murmuring, "Nice doggie. Here, boy. Nice, doggie."

Nero spat the thing at him. He picked it up warily and leapt back from those alarming teeth, then examined his prize.

"It's a ten-pound note!" he exclaimed.

The hounds were off on another frenzied chase. With their ropes entwined, they could not run as far as they wanted. They strained at their leashes, yapping.

"Here, you take one lead," Prance said, and began untangling the ropes.

Eventually each of them had one lead. The hounds immediately took off in two separate directions, pulling a reluctant Prance and Coffen after them.

"Another note!" Coffen exclaimed.

"Mine has one, too!" Prance called.

Other notes were seen blowing through the meadow. Each fresh breeze sent the hounds off on a merry chase. When ten notes had been collected, the hounds returned to the valise and began attacking it with renewed vigor.

"Did the highwayman drop the valise, I wonder, and

all Susan's money is out floating on the breeze?" Prance asked.

"Dashed careless of him. There'd ought to be a lot more bills floating around if that is what happened." Coffen's face pinched with the effort of thought. "What it is," he said a moment later, "the kidnapper smelled the vanilla and figured out what I was up to. He dumped the money into something—his jacket or a horse blanket—and left the valise and a few bills to distract the blood-hounds."

"A clever stunt," Prance said. "I believe you're right, Pattle. The question is, what do we do next?"

Coffen lifted his nose and sniffed the breeze, looked at the trees to confirm which way the wind blew, and said, "We go that way." He pointed toward East Grinstead. "The hounds will soon lose the scent of the valise. The wind is blowing from Grinstead, blowing the smell away from them. If they pick up the scent in that direction, we follow them."

"I doubt the scent will be on the bills."

"Dogs can smell out the weakest scent a mile away. My old hound, Jackie, used to go into conniptions when Mrs. Armstead took a roast out of the oven. She lived two miles away."

"Who is to say the kidnapper went toward Grinstead?"

"He didn't come out by the forest road where we were waiting for Otto. He wouldn't bother going deep into the forest after he'd got rid of Luten. If he went the other direction, he's heading for Appleby Court. I doubt he'd do that. It's the shepherd's hut I'm thinking of. He might have hidden the blunt there, or thereabouts."

"He would know by now that Hodden suspects the hut."

"Hodden hasn't got a guard on it. He thinks Jeremy was the highwayman. The hut is safe as a church. Mind you, I'm not saying it's in the hut. That area would be handy for him, is all I mean. Out of the way. He might have dumped the blunt into the stream to kill the smell."

Prance, having nothing better to put forward, said, "Let us go."

The hounds were reluctant to leave. Between the taste of the leather valise and the sweet attraction of vanilla, they were rapidly chewing the corners of the case to shreds. It took some minutes to convince them their job was not done.

They left the clearing and began tracking rather at random through the forest. It was clear they had lost the scent.

When they came out of the forest onto the main road, Prance said, "Now what? Do we go on to the hut, despite the hounds' lack of interest in it?"

"Might as well have a look while we're this close."

He waved the vanilla-scented handkerchief under the dogs' noses. For half a mile they continued with no encouraging signs. Suddenly Nero began to sniff the ground with a renewed interest. Caesar soon took up the scent. The two sleek animals left the road, ran behind the hedgerow that edged the road, and began to run faster, faster, with Coffen and Prance keeping pace on their mounts. Their route was parallel to the road, hidden by the hedgerow.

"I can't believe it worked!" Prance exclaimed, and murmured something about the thin line between idiocy and genius.

"We'd best stop and make some plans," Coffen said, and drew to a halt.

"Regarding what we do when we reach our destination, you mean?"

"About what we do when we find the bounder."

"That's what I said. Discretion will be called for."

"Aye, the more of it the better. We'll slip up on him with our pistols drawn. The hounds will help."

"Not they! They'll eat the blunt. They seem to like vanilla."

When they came to a crossing in the road, Coffen peered around to get the lay of the land. "There's the hut ahead!" he exclaimed. "On the far side of the stream."

"The hounds don't seem interested. They're not crossing the stream."

"See where they go. We'll follow them."

After another twenty yards, the hounds plowed into the stream.

"The crafty devil has used the stream to kill his scent!" Prance exclaimed. "We've lost him now."

"Caesar and Nero will pick up the smell on t'other side," Coffen assured him, and waded his mount through the water, with Prance beside him.

The hounds began sniffing the ground on the other side and soon took up the trail again.

"That's Prissy Trueheart's little cottage," Prance said a moment later. The little thatched cottage with leaded windows looked innocent in the moonlight. A few lights burned on the ground floor.

"It is, and the lads are heading straight for it. Now, why is it lit up when you said she'd left? She must still be there."

"Prissy Trueheart! Surely she can't be behind this. Pattle, you don't suppose Blackmore—"

"At the bottom of the whole thing, I shouldn't wonder. Never cared for him above half. An oiler."

"How embarrassing! I wish I weren't here," Prance said on a disillusioned sigh. "What do you say we go fetch Hodden?"

"They might make their getaway. I say we go in and arrest them. I'll hold them while you go for Hodden.

Come now, Prance, show your mettle!" Coffen said severely. When this failed to sway him, he added slyly, "Think of all the glory you'll be trailing when you go back to London."

This was indeed a consideration. And besides, it was only Blackmore and a female against two men and two large, slavering dogs. They rode toward the back of the house. A dark mount was tied to the mulberry tree in the backyard.

"You're right," Prance said. "Carry on, Pattle. I am right behind you."

"I'd rather have you by my side. We'll go in the back door, take 'em by surprise."

"There might be a servant in the kitchen. There's a light on."

"We'll peek in the window."

Coffen dismounted and crept up to the window. Through the faded lace curtain he saw two people sitting at a table—a man and a woman. The man's back was to him. The woman might have been Prissy. The flickering light of one lamp wasn't bright enough to be certain, but she was definitely a brunette.

The hounds were becoming impatient with this dallying way of going on. One of them lifted his forepaws to the windowsill beside Coffen and peered in. Something caused him to emit a yelp of excitement. Coffen clamped his hand over the dog's mouth.

It was no good. The people inside had heard it. The man jumped up and ran to the back door. There was scarcely time to leap behind a rain barrel before the door opened and he peeked out. He looked all around and went back in.

Prance peered out from behind the mulberry tree. "He was wearing a mask!" he exclaimed. "It must be the highwayman."

"Why was he wearing a mask in the house—or did he put it on to look out the door? Cautious fellow. Let's go, before he barricades the door."

Coffen went quietly to the door at a stooping gait, due to having to muzzle Caesar with his fingers, as he had forgotten to provide the hounds with muzzles. The dogs were becoming excited. Coffen tried the door and found it locked. Prance breathed a great sigh of relief. This gave them an excellent excuse to go and fetch Hodden. Before he could voice this suggestion, Coffen raised his pistol, there was a terrific explosion, and the door flew open. He went storming into the kitchen. Prance swallowed down his anxiety and went after him.

When he saw the two hounds take a flying leap at Blackmore—he had taken off his mask—Prance breathed another sigh of relief.

"We know you've got the blunt, Blackmore," Coffen said, in his usual calm voice. "Lie down on the floor. You, too, Miss Trueheart. I'm going to tie you up, and Prance is going to fetch Hodden."

Blackmore lifted his hand; it held a pistol.

"Don't be a fool, Blackmore," Prance said in a quavering voice. "Those hounds will tear you limb from limb."

Blackmore laughed. It occurred to Prance at that instant that the hounds, far from tearing Blackmore limb from limb, were licking his fingers and showing other signs of affection.

"I don't think so, Prance," he replied. "I've known these fellows since they were pups. I sold 'em to Lafferty. Sic 'em, Caesar, Nero."

The dogs turned. Deep, dangerous growls began to emanate from their throats. Their hackles rose menacingly. There was a fearsome display of long, pointed teeth. Blackmore grabbed their ropes in his left hand to restrain them.

"*Point non plus,* gentlemen," he said. "Would you prefer a clean bullet or a messy end?"

Prance's pistol clattered to the floor. He took out a handkerchief and patted his moist brow with trembling fingers. Prissy darted forward, snatched up the gun, and pointed it at them.

"Kill them," she said to Blackmore.

"I shouldn't do that if I were you. Everyone knows we're here," Coffen lied blandly. "The jig is up, Blackmore." They faced each other, each pointing a pistol at the other.

Blackmore stood like a statue, his steely eyes narrowed in thought. The dogs growled and strained at their leashes. "I think not, Pattle. I call your bluff."

"Suit yourself," Pattle said. His left hand shot out and snatched the pistol out of Prissy's hand. He pointed the two pistols at Blackmore, one in either hand. His hands weren't even trembling. Prance told himself Coffen was too unimaginative to be afraid, but he didn't really believe it. Coffen had actually a better imagination than any of them. He often came up with ideas. It was a strange and lowering thought to admit that Coffen Pattle was as brave as a lion.

"Shoot him," Prissy said again to Blackmore. Her voice rose in panic. "Go on, what are you waiting for? They can only hang you once. You've already killed Soames."

Blackmore's voice lashed out like a whip. "Shut up, you fool!"

Prance was seized with the fear he was going to faint and half wished he would. But then the dogs would devour him. It was no fit death for a gentleman.

"If you haven't the bottom for it, I'll do it myself,"

Prissy said, and grabbed the pistol from Blackmore's hand. Her own hand was steady. She seemed familiar with guns.

"Go ahead," Blackmore said. "I suggest you begin with Pattle. He seems the more dangerous of the pair."

She lifted the gun and pointed it at Coffen. Before she could fire, Coffen pulled the trigger of his weapon and the gun flew out of her hand, to clatter on the floor at her feet.

Blackmore unleashed the dogs. One leapt at Coffen, the other at Prance. It went against the grain with Coffen to shoot a dog. He loved dogs, but he loved his life more. He dropped the guns and tried to get hold of the rope to choke the attacking hound into obedience. Meanwhile, Prissy was making a great clamor, holding her hand and crying and shouting curses at Blackmore, who stood smiling wanly at the fracas before him.

The other dog—Nero, it was—had leapt on Prance. The force of the two paws against his chest knocked Prance to the floor, with the dog yelping in his face, with those great, long teeth flashing. Staring an extremely degrading and painful death in the face, Prance found the courage to defend himself. He put his two hands around the dog's throat and held it off at arm's length with the strength of desperation. He knew if he avoided being eaten alive by dogs, he was looking at death by pistol. The pistol was faster and cleaner. He struggled on.

They had reached this impasse when Luten, holding a pistol, stepped into the kitchen. Behind him reared the stalwart frame of Rufus Stockwell. He also held a gun. It looked like a whole army behind Stockwell, although it was actually only Simon, Luten's valet, and a groom. Stockwell and Simon ran forward and subdued the hounds. Rufus said simply, "Down, boys," and they subsided to docility. He took them outdoors and tied them to the mulberry tree.

Blackmore conceded defeat gracefully. His gaze ran over the assembled men. He turned to Prance, who had picked himself up from the floor.

"You will see they use a silken rope for my execution, Prance," he said. "We gentlemen must stick together."

Prance, restored to arrogance, said, "I fear I cannot oblige you, Blackmore. You have put yourself beyond the pale."

"Where's the money, Blackmore?" Coffen asked.

"In the cupboard. Where else would one keep vanilla?" he asked, and strolled out, with Stockwell's pistol nudging his spine.

Prance, watching, admired Blackmore's sangfroid. Perhaps he did deserve a silken rope after all.

Chapter Twenty-five

Otto dozed in an easy chair by the cold grate. An expression of ease sat on his lined face. Corinne felt obliged to deliver the necessary scold to Susan for the fright she had given them all, before they could get down to more interesting talk.

"I had no choice." Susan pouted. "Rufus simply refused to marry me, no matter how often I told him the money didn't matter. And it was not that he didn't love me, for I knew he did. One can always tell."

"How did you know?" Corinne asked, and listened more closely to that answer than to any other.

"Oh, *you* know. His face got all red when I flirted with him. He used to make excuses to ride out and accidentally meet me when he saw me leave for the village. Stuttering and stammering and blushing. You know."

This was no help to Corinne at all. She realized that the sophisticated Luten would no more be guilty of these rustic intimations of love than he would wear a soiled shirt. Nor would she be comfortable flirting with him. Theirs was a different sort of romance.

"So you assembled your trousseau and decided to foist yourself on him," she said.

"I thought he would have to marry me if I could contrive to spend a night under his roof. I packed a lunch in

208

my sewing basket and told Mrs. Malboeuf I was going to the orchard."

"How did the basket end up in the apple tree?"

"I had to wait ever so long to sneak into Greenleigh. Mrs. Dorman was doing the washing that day and kept going into the yard. By the time she was finished, I had eaten the lunch, so I just chucked the basket up into the tree. I didn't want to leave it on the ground. The Jamieson boys sometimes play in the orchard, and they are such mischievous fellows, I was afraid they would destroy it or even steal it."

"The basket is safe in your room," Corinne assured her.

"Oh, good. Now, where was I? Oh yes, it was very scary and uncomfortable all alone in the attic, but luckily I fell asleep while reading that book you sent me. Then at dawn when I felt I was compromised, I went down to Rufus's room to tell him I had been there all night. He was *angry* with me," she said, greatly vexed at his lack of consideration. "He only thought of himself, saying everyone would put it in *his* dish and think he was after my money. I very nearly gave up on him, after all the trouble I had gone to and he didn't appreciate it. But instead I cried, and he said he would see what we could do. You ought to try tears if you are having trouble bringing Luten up to scratch, Corinne," she added with a sly smile that showed she had lost the last vestige of girlhood.

"I never thought of that," Corinne said, chewing back a grin at the absurdity of it. Luten would tell her to stop being a watering pot and pull herself together. And she would think the better of him for it. She didn't want such a biddable husband as Rufus Stockwell.

Susan continued her tale. "Rufus told Mrs. Dorman he was hunting bats in the attic to explain any little noises I might make and to make an excuse to spend some time with me, for it was horrid up there all alone. He was

209

frightened to death when you and Luten called on him. He feared Luten was going to issue a challenge. After that, he just went about his work on the farm as usual during the day and only visited me at night. I told him he need not worry about Luten. He took no interest in my affairs," she finished, with an angry sniff.

"Why had you been writing to Luten recently? Was it to do with marrying Rufus?"

"I wanted Luten to tell Rufus it was all right to marry me. I wrote to Luten and told him I had to speak to him most urgently and asked him to come to Appleby. He wrote back that my allowance was adequate and that if I really required an increase, I must speak to Otto. I wrote again and told him it was not about money, it was practically a matter of life and death, but still he did not come. I expect it was about then your pearls were stolen, and he was busy finding them for you."

"Yes, it was," Corinne said. So that was why Luten spoke of Susan's disappearance weighing on his conscience, and why he wore that strained, white face. Because he felt he had forsaken her in her dire trouble, and if he had come, she would be safe at home. Perhaps he even worried that she had thrown herself into a river.

When Susan went on to apologize for having to cut three inches off the bottom of that sprigged muslin gown Rufus had picked up in error in the dark, Corinne was not in a mood to scold.

"Naturally you would not want to be tripping on the hem. As long as my cashmere shawl is all right—"

"Mrs. Dorman thinks she can get the cocoa stains out. And the little hole where I caught it on a nail will hardly show once it is mended. Oh, and I fear I broke that little mirror Prance gave you. Rufus accidentally stepped on it."

"It is really of no importance at all," Corinne said, "but

I notice you are not wearing the little hand ring I sent you, nor was it in your room. Have you lost it?"

She gave a simpering smile. "I gave it to Rufus at the May Day party," she said. "He was admiring it one day when I went to Greenleigh pretending Mrs. Malboeuf needed eggs for a cake. He wouldn't accept it at first, but I told him the clasped hands made it a friendship ring, and if he wanted to be my friend, he must accept it. So he did. He bought a silver chain and wears it around his neck, next to his heart."

From there the conversation turned to the wedding and trousseau. "I notice you have bought some new linen," Corinne said.

"I need ever so many things. I shall be rid of Mrs. Malboeuf and have Mrs. Dorman be our housekeeper here at Appleby. It did not seem worthwhile finding someone to replace Malboeuf for a few months. I want to consult Rufus about what sort of carpets and curtains and things he would like before I replace them. It will be such fun, like playing house."

A rosy dawn was showing in the eastern sky when the gentlemen returned to Appleby Court. The sound of footsteps sent the ladies racing into the hall to demand an accounting of what had been going on.

Chapter Twenty-six

Tobin, who had not gone to bed on this momentous night, went to the kitchen to rouse Mrs. Malboeuf to make coffee and sandwiches, and to give her a hand.

"Did you get my money?" Susan asked Luten.

He dumped the horse blanket on the sofa table. Bills tumbled out in heaps. "A few pounds might be blowing around the meadow. We haven't counted it," he said.

Rufus made a mental note to scour the meadow in the morning. Otto roused himself and began checking to see that each bill did indeed have a neatly hidden hole in its center, though it was not really important now. This done, he began to assemble the bills into neat piles for counting.

"Who had it?" Corinne asked.

"Blackmore and Prissy Trueheart," Coffen announced.

"Who is Prissy Trueheart?" Susan asked.

"Mrs. Spencer."

The story was told, with suitable *ooh*s and *ah*s and praise for everyone's bravery. Prance felt insufficient concern was shown for his close brush with death, but he was busy working it up into a harrowing tale for the more prestigious drawing rooms of London and let the others take their share of credit.

"So the highwayman was Blackmore?" Corinne asked.

"Eventually," Luten said wearily, and poured himself a glass of wine.

"Don't be tarsome, Luten. I'll explain," Coffen said. "It was Blackmore and Prissy. It started out being Prissy, dressed up in trousers. She had sunk to that, imagine! She used to be one of the lights of the London stage."

"Sic transit gloria mundi," Prance said.

"I daresay one would get sick of it," Coffen said. "It turns out her papa and brother are both scamps, so she comes by her dishonesty honestly. She made the mistake of holding up Blackmore one night. He soon outwitted her and had her mask off."

"And a few other items of apparel, I shouldn't wonder," Prance said coyly.

Coffen frowned. "Behave yourself, Reg. There's ladies present. Before you could say Jack Robinson, they were in league. When Prissy told him how easy it was, Blackmore took over the actual robbing. All a hum, that business of him inheriting from a Scottish aunt. It was stolen rhino he was using to fix up the Hall. 'Twas Blackmore who held us up, Corinne. Got my watch back." He drew it out and smiled at it before continuing.

"Prissy had it hidden with a bunch of other things to take to London. She is the Mrs. Bewley who hawked the other items. Hodden mentioned her; she said she was from up north somewhere. They didn't plan to rob any more coaches. Since Jeremy was blamed for it, they figured it was a good time to stop. Their scheme was to make one last haul by stealing Susan's ransom money, then dart off to London with their pockets jingling."

He gazed fondly at his watch again. Prance shivered in revulsion. He despised turnip watches. One might as well carry a clock and have done with it.

"Prissy occasionally handled a job by herself when Blackmore was at a dinner party or what have you, to

213

make him look innocent," Coffen continued. "And he did the same for her. Take it up and down and all around, a tidy little racket they had going."

"Blackmore's servant told him that Mr. Marchbank was delivering the money tonight?" Corinne asked.

Prance nodded. "Just so. He sent her down, pretending he wanted to learn if there was any news of Susan. Blackmore knew the very spot, by the blasted oak, and went early, though not so early as Luten. He did not know that Luten planned to be there, nor did he ever realize that he was resting in the arms of Morpheus behind the tree the whole time."

Coffen was on his feet. "Now, see here, Prance, that is going a good deal too far. Luten wasn't with a woman. He was knocked out cold."

"Morpheus is a he, my dear ignoramus. The *us* ending would have told you so, had you spent more than a few weeks at Cambridge."

"A he! This goes from bad to worse!"

"Sleep, Coffen."

"I ain't tired. Luten, are you going to sit there and let him—"

"Morpheus is just another word for sleep. *C'est tout,*" Prance said, and tossed his hands up in resignation for the obtuseness of Pattle.

"Well, why the devil didn't you say so?" Coffen grumbled. "And how did the laudanum get into his coffee anyhow, I should like to know."

"Peggy did it for me," Susan explained, smiling at her cleverness. "I asked her to, when I learned that Luten planned to unmask Rufus when he went to collect my money."

"May I continue?" Prance asked, with heavy irony.

"Go ahead, but no more of that funny talk," Coffen warned.

"Now, where was I? When Stockwell had collected the money, Blackmore waited until he saw which route he was taking out of the forest, then slipped out to the road by a shorter route and was waiting for him. He feared the poachers might come to Rufus's help if he did it in the forest. Blackmore knows the forest like the back of his hand from his highwayman activities. Excellent hiding there, of course."

The sandwiches and coffee arrived, and they all discussed their adventure until the food and drink were gone.

A rosy glow lit the sky when Tobin came to assist Otto to bed. Rufus blushingly asked Susan if she would like to see him to the door, and she was not tardy to oblige him. They stepped outside for maximum privacy.

Coffen rose, stretched, and said, "I'm for the feather tick. We've earned our rest. We can all hang our heads high. We rescued Susan. When will we be getting back to London, folks? We'll not make the trip after dark, I trust?"

"Let us have one day to rest and leave tomorrow morning," Prance said. "We are in no shape to travel today."

"I promised Susan I would spend a few days with her to help her with her trousseau and wedding plans," Corinne said.

Luten added, "I told Hodden I would call on him tomorrow and help him with his report. I'll attend Jeremy's funeral as well."

"We should all stay for that," Coffen said. He was in a pensive mood. He had thought he would be broken-hearted at Susan's betrothal to Rufus, but all things considered, he was relieved. Susan was no longer a nice, simple girl. A devilish hoyden, she had become, putting everyone through such an ordeal, just to foist herself on a fellow who didn't want her when all was said and done. The sliest lady in the parish.

Prance sat massaging his chin. "As we are to remain a few days, I shall see who inherits Blackmore Hall. There are a few items there I shouldn't mind buying. That *scrivanìa* would just suit my bedroom."

"That what?" Coffen asked.

"Desk, Coffen."

"You already have one. What do you want another for?"

"For a sculpture," Prance said, thinking he was delivering a leveler. "Pity Angelica's marvelous mural couldn't be removed and sent to London, but the thing cannot be done." He stretched, looked at Coffen, and said, "Time for bed."

"It's too late to go to bed, and too early to get up."

"True, but let us be nice and leave these two lovebirds to make up their differences."

"What differences?" Coffen asked, in his usual blunt way.

Prance took him by the elbow and led him from the room. "You have not observed the chill in the air since Luten failed to come up to scratch in time for my party?"

"Nothing of the sort. You can't expect a fellow to shackle himself for life just to give a point to one of your parties."

"You are putting the cart before the horse. I planned the party because it was clear as glass that Luten was on the point of proposing."

"You'd ought to have waited until he did it."

"I shall, next time. Oh, I know I said I would not give them another party, but when true love calls, I fly to do her bidding. Besides, I have had a stunning idea for a theme. Tell me what you think of it, Pattle. A Venetian ball, with all the guests to dress in elaborate Italian out-fits, with those marvelous masks."

"You'll beggar yourself with all these parties."

"It won't be expensive. It will just cost rather a lot. Oh dear, I have been spending too much time with you."

"Feeling's mutual," Coffen snipped.

"No offense intended, dear boy. This will be no ordi-nary masquerade. No dominoes allowed, absolutely! I wonder, now, if it would be possible to contrive some miniature resemblance of the famous bronze horses of Saint Mark's to grace the foyer."

"Why not throw in the Grand Canal while you're about it?"

"What a splendid idea! I begin to see this should be held out of doors, near water. A gondola or two to pole the guests up and down. How do I come up with these ideas?"

"*Why* do you come up with them?"

Their voices trailed off to silence as they mounted the stairs. In the saloon, Luten looked uncertainly at Corinne, then rose to join her on the sofa.

"I expect you're wondering why I failed to offer before Prance's ball," he said uncertainly.

"Offer what?" she asked, with an air of disinterest.

"To marry you. You heard what Prance said."

"I wasn't listening." She raised her hand and yawned daintily into her fingers. "My, how late it is. We should go upstairs, too."

Luten took a deep breath and plunged into his explana-tion. "Susan and I have been corresponding on and off since my visit last February. She was pestering me about a dozen things that are really Otto's concern, not mine. When the letters became a nuisance, I tapered off on my replies. I thought she had stopped writing, until I had a letter from her a few weeks ago."

217

"Susan told me about writing to you. I know you have been feeling guilty for not coming."

"I didn't even answer her last letter. It came the day before Prance's party. When I heard she had disappeared . . . Well, you can imagine how I felt. In her second to last letter she mentioned that she wanted to get married. I wrote back at once approving the idea, as it would give her a new interest. Then she wrote telling me she was delighted that I agreed and asking when I could come to arrange the details—the date, the marriage settlement, and so on."

He threw out his hands helplessly. "Not a mention of Rufus Stockwell. It sounded as if she thought *I* was to be the bridegroom. I deduced I had been overly enthusiastic in my reply. Actually, she was trying to flirt with me last February, when I stopped for a night. I didn't want to throw our happiness in her face at that moment, when she was vulnerable—or so I thought, egotistical ass that I am. When I got Soames's note at the party, I thought . . . I hardly know what. Suicide occurred as one possibility, though I couldn't see her flinging herself into a pond without leaving a note to make me aware of my treachery."

"So that's why you were so eager to search her room and to conceal the trousseau."

"And most of all, to find her, so I wouldn't have to go through life feeling like a murderer. My nerves have been overwrought. If I have behaved badly, and I know I have . . ." A shadow of doubt clouded the eyes that gazed at her questioningly.

"No worse than usual," she said, shaking her head ruefully. Dear, kind Luten, trying to look after them all and not hurt anyone. And half-ashamed of his kindness. "You hadn't heard of her disappearance until halfway through the ball, however," she reminded him. "You knew about the party for a week before receiving Susan's last letter and didn't offer for me. You weren't sure you wanted to marry me."

"Of course I was sure! My fear was that you'd let Prance bullock you into a betrothal because of his party. If you accepted me, I wanted it to be because you loved me. I offered for you once before, if you recall, and you laughed in my face. I thought you cared for me that time and was wrong."

"What a long memory you have, elephant! And it wasn't a laugh, exactly. More of a nervous giggle. You caught me quite off guard."

"I put you on notice now, Countess." He placed his hands on her shoulders and drew her into his arms. "Prepare yourself to receive an offer before we leave Appleby Court."

She was caught in the glitter of his dark diamond eyes as his head descended and their lips brushed. A tingle started somewhere in her chest and fanned out to her whole body as his arms crushed her against him and the hot silk of his lips firmed to a kiss of passion.

Prance tiptoed back downstairs to eavesdrop on the proposal. He was not a voyeur, he assured himself. If they were bickering, he would postpone the Venetian ball until some other grand occasion arose. Hearing only the sound of silence, he risked peering around the doorjamb into the saloon. He watched, fascinated, as Luten behaved in quite a naughty manner, and Corinne did not call him to account as she ought either.

These ladies! Corinne would make a satisfactory enough wife, but Susan! He pitied Rufus with all his heart. The shrew would ride roughshod over him. She had already informed him that he would remove to Appleby and hire Greenleigh out to some elderly couple with no pretty daughters but not sell it. She wanted it for their

219

daughter. Their son, of course, would inherit Appleby Court. She had quite forgotten to mention Oakhurst, which was now hers as well.

He waited quite five minutes, and when still the proposal had not been made, though their behavior certainly warranted it, he turned and went upstairs to bed, planning their second engagement party. The venue was troublesome. He had a river on his country estate, but one could hardly invite half of polite London there. Berkeley Square, of course, had no water for the Grand Canal.

Perhaps a carpenter could construct a sort of large aqueduct in the ballroom. But then there would not be room for the gondolas. Unless he made miniature ones . . . He would sleep on it. Important decisions should not be made without due consideration.